CONTENTS

PART FIVE: CONTEXTS AND CRITICAL DEBATES

PART SIX: GRADE BOOSTER

ESSENTIAL STUDY TOOLS

HOW TO STUDY *WUTHERING HEIGHTS*

These Notes can be used in a range of ways to help you read, study and (where relevant) revise for your exam or assessment.

READING THE NOVEL

Read the novel once, fairly quickly, for pleasure. This will give you a good sense of the over-arching shape of the **narrative**, and a good feel for the highs and lows of the action, the pace and tone, and the sequence in which information is withheld or revealed. You could ask yourself:

- How do individual characters change or develop? How do my own responses to them change?
- From whose point of view is the novel told? Does this change or remain the same?
- Are the events presented chronologically, or is the time scheme altered in some way?
- What impression do the locations and settings, such as the Yorkshire moors, make on my reading and response to the text?
- What sort of language, style and form am I aware of as the novel progresses? Does Brontë paint detail precisely, or is there deliberate vagueness or ambiguity – or both? Does she use imagery, or recurring motifs and **symbols**?

On your second reading, make detailed notes around the key areas highlighted above and in the Assessment Objectives, such as form, language, structure (AO2), links and connections to other texts (AO3) and the context/background for the novel (AO4). These may seem quite demanding, but these Notes will suggest particular elements to explore or jot down.

> **GRADE BOOSTER** **A02**
>
> Finding good quotations to support your interpretation of the characters will greatly enhance and strengthen your points.

INTERPRETING OR CRITIQUING THE NOVEL

Although it's not helpful to think in terms of the novel being 'good' or 'bad', you should consider the different ways the novel can be read. How have critics responded to it? Do their views match yours – or do you take a different viewpoint? Are there different ways you can interpret specific events, characters or settings? This is a key aspect in AO3, and it can be helpful to keep a log of your responses and the various perspectives which are expressed both by established critics, and also by classmates, your teacher, or other readers.

REFERENCES AND SOURCES

You will be expected to draw on critics' comments, or refer to source information from the period or the present. Make sure you make accurate, clear notes of writers or sources you have used, for example noting down titles of works, authors' names, website addresses, dates, etc. You may not have to reference all these things when you respond to a text, but knowing the source of your information will allow you to go back to it, if need be – and to check its accuracy and relevance.

REVISING FOR AND RESPONDING TO AN ASSESSED TASK OR EXAM QUESTION

The structure and the contents of these Notes are designed to help to give you the relevant information or ideas you need to answer tasks you have been set. First, work out the key words or ideas from the task (for example, 'form', 'Volume I, Chapter IX', 'Heathcliff', etc.), then read the relevant parts of the Notes that relate to these terms or words, selecting what is useful for revision or written response. Then, turn to **Part Six: Grade Booster** for help in formulating your actual response.

WUTHERING HEIGHTS IN CONTEXT

EMILY BRONTË: LIFE AND TIMES

30 July 1818 Emily Brontë born at Thornton in Bradford, the fifth of six children. Mary Shelley publishes *Frankenstein*

1820 Family move to Haworth to the parsonage where Patrick Brontë was made curate

1821 Mother dies and Emily and three older sisters sent to clergy school

1825 Two older sisters Maria and Elizabeth die of TB

1830s Gothic Revival period in architecture: British Houses of Parliament built; 1832 Reform Act on women's suffrage passed

1837 Queen Victoria crowned

1845–1860 Enclosure Acts passed in Parliament

1846 Charlotte, Emily and Anne publish their poems under the names of Currer, Ellis and Acton Bell

1847 *Wuthering Heights* published

1848 Beginnings of feminist movement evident in England. Emily Brontë dies

Emily Brontë
from a painting of a family group by Branwell Brontë

CONTEXT **A03**

It was not uncommon in Victorian times for authors to adopt a pseudonym – Dickens, for example, famously used the name Boz, and Thackeray called himself Titmarsh.

CHECK THE BOOK **A03**

Emily's sister Charlotte's reply to Southey, which attempts to clarify the 'business of a woman's life', makes reference to the 'angel in the house', a term which has since been taken up by contemporary feminist critics Sandra Gilbert and Susan Gubar, most notably in their collection of essays *The Madwoman in the Attic: The Woman Writer and the Nineteenth-Century Literary Imagination* (1979).

WUTHERING HEIGHTS: A REVOLUTIONARY NOVEL?

Wuthering Heights is Emily Brontë's only novel and it was published together with her sister Anne's novel *Agnes Grey* in December 1847. The sisters decided to use the same deliberately masculine-sounding **pseudonyms** they had used a year earlier when they published their book of poetry under the title *Poems by Currer, Ellis and Acton Bell*. This was because, as women writers, they wanted their poetry to receive due critical attention.

As their elder sister Charlotte Brontë explained: 'We had a vague impression that authoresses are liable to be looked on with prejudice' (Biographical Notice in *Wuthering Heights*, p. xliv). The identity of the authors was only revealed by Charlotte when she revised the text of *Wuthering Heights* and added her preface to the second edition, published in 1850, two years after Emily Brontë's death. Most modern editions of the novel include Charlotte Brontë's prefaces.

The Brontë sisters were right to be concerned: some readers reacted negatively to Charlotte's revelation that Ellis Bell, the author of *Wuthering Heights*, was in fact a woman. Some of these prejudices appear clearly in the correspondence between Charlotte Brontë and the famous poet Robert Southey, who asserted: 'Literature cannot be the business of a woman's life, and it ought not to be.' It is possible to argue therefore that *Wuthering Heights* simultaneously challenged Victorian ideas about what was proper for literature and what was proper for a woman.

SETTING

The novel is set in the bleak moorside of Yorkshire, and the geography of the novel can be considered as a character itself. The desolate landscape is difficult to negotiate, and especially given to harsh weather. This acts as a **metaphor** for the uncertain moral landscape which the characters inhabit. The **eponymous** house, Wuthering Heights, is believed to be based on a Yeoman house called High Sunderland which can be found near Law Hill, the school near Halifax where Emily taught in 1838. Thrushcross Grange is believed to be based upon an amalgamation of Shibden Hall, also near Halifax, and Ponden Hall near Stanbury. The two locations are **structural oppositions**, in that Wuthering Heights is isolated, dark and forbidding, and set upon the hillside, whereas Thrushcross Grange is more sunny, and located in the valley.

Although the two locations are only four miles apart, the characters frequently miss their way going between the two and the journey from one to the other is considered perilous and fraught. Both sites are representative of a certain social status, and Heathcliff, the outsider, ends up welcome in neither. The bleakly isolated setting and the difficulty of mobility and access are revealing of many of the novel's themes of social class, exclusion, property and identity. The descriptions of the setting are in direct contrast with the **Romantic** view of the open landscape as **sublime** and uplifting.

KEY THEMES AND ISSUES

The key themes in *Wuthering Heights* are childhood; the eternal nature of love; social and class mobility; knowledge; the conflict between culture and nature; property and belonging; morality; and dreams. Of these, the conflict between culture and nature forms the structural spine of the novel and is broadly represented by the two houses, Thrushcross Grange and Wuthering Heights respectively.

The key issues are repetition and the uncanny; psychology and character; social mobility and property; education; religion; nostalgia; and authenticity. The landscape is a central motif and operates as a key metaphor for character, morality and psychological equilibrium. Animal imagery also functions to describe human frailty or moral deficiency.

GRADE BOOSTER A02

Brontë's use of hostile weather conditions and bleak settings reflects the social hardships of the nineteenth century, and the surly natures of the characters in this novel. The literary term for this relationship between landscape description and themes is a **pathetic fallacy**. Examiners will be impressed if you can explain this term and show its effects.

CONTEXT A03

A ruined farmhouse known as Top Withens (also Top Withins), which lies on the Pennine Way east of Withins Heights and within walking distance of the parsonage, bears a plaque from the Brontë Society which reads: 'This farmhouse has been associated with Wuthering Heights, the Earnshaw home in Emily Brontë's novel. The buildings, even when complete, bore no resemblance to the house she described, but the situation may have been in her mind when she wrote of the moorland setting of the Heights' (Brontë Society, 1964). This plaque was placed here in response to many enquiries.

CONTEXT A03

Emily Brontë and her siblings lived isolated lives in the parsonage at Haworth. In the biographical notice which prefaces most editions of the text, Charlotte Brontë explains that they took their chief enjoyment from stories that they invented for each other, most famously the sagas of the mythical island of Gondal which inspired their later poetry.

THE GOTHIC GENRE

The **Gothic** is a style of literature which combines horror and romance. It typically features supernatural encounters, graveyards, ghosts, desolate landscapes and crumbling ruins, in order to convey the effect of pleasurable terror. The Gothic Romance was a form of literature popular in the late eighteenth and nineteenth centuries. It generally dealt with the supernatural and the fantastic.

Haunted by ghosts and hallucinations, *Wuthering Heights* can be described as a Gothic novel. Heathcliff's profound passion and desire for Catherine, which extends beyond the grave and transcends the conventional boundaries of class and time, clearly places Gothic ideas at the heart of the novel. *Wuthering Heights* is a highly provoking novel which is full of contradictions, which defies stable readings, and which is full of unresolved puzzles, unexplained dreams and unquiet ghosts.

SOCIAL CONTEXT

Contemporary readers of *Wuthering Heights* would have been familiar with stories like that of Heathcliff being a foundling from the port of Liverpool. Orphans and child beggars were a common social problem. Heathcliff's uncertain origins can be read as a realistic account of the social upheavals of the mid nineteenth century, which saw mass unemployment as a result of the Industrial Revolution, and the decay of a rural lifestyle in the face of increased urbanisation and new technology.

CHECK THE BOOK A03

Mrs Gaskell's *The Life of Charlotte Brontë*, first published in 1857, provides a useful account of the life of a woman writer in the nineteenth century.

The Industrial Revolution dramatically changed the social structure in Britain. Prior to industrialisation, three quarters of Britain's population lived in the countryside, working in agriculture or as skilled craftsmen. The new enclosure laws of 1845–82 meant that many farmers could no longer afford to farm the land. The factories were capable of producing far more, and far more quickly, than a hand-weaver. This meant that families were forced to move to the towns to work in the factories, where they toiled for long hours and were paid very little money. Family life was eroded, people could no longer sustain themselves, and there was widespread poverty and unrest.

FAMILY TREE

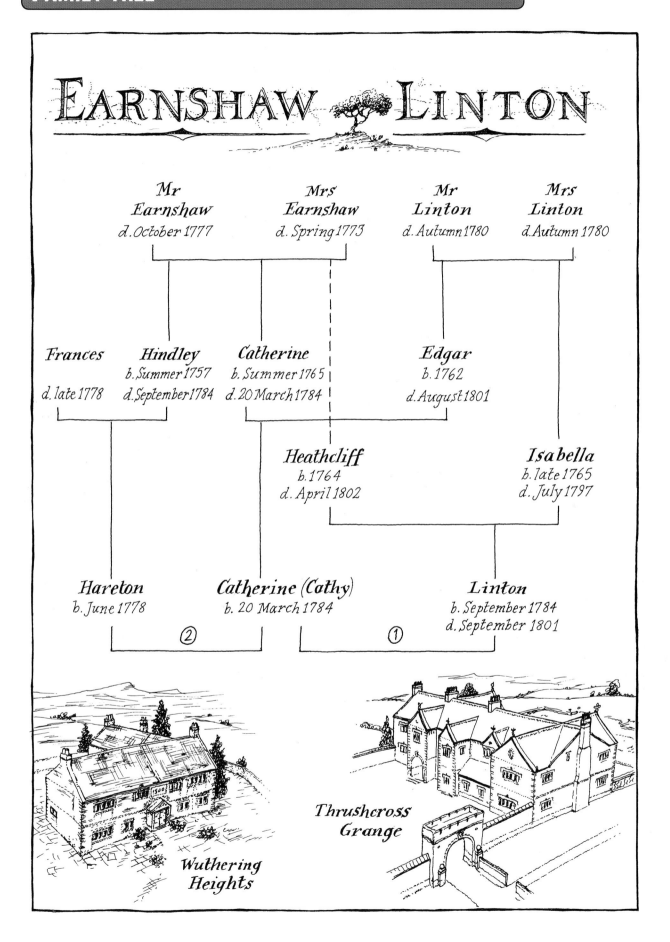

EARNSHAW LINTON

Mr Earnshaw
d. October 1777

Mrs Earnshaw
d. Spring 1773

Mr Linton
d. Autumn 1780

Mrs Linton
d. Autumn 1780

Frances
d. late 1778

Hindley
b. Summer 1757
d. September 1784

Catherine
b. Summer 1765
d. 20 March 1784

Edgar
b. 1762
d. August 1801

Heathcliff
b. 1764
d. April 1802

Isabella
b. late 1765
d. July 1797

Hareton
b. June 1778

Catherine (Cathy)
b. 20 March 1784

Linton
b. September 1784
d. September 1801

②

①

Wuthering Heights

Thrushcross Grange

SYNOPSIS

THE BEGINNING

The novel famously opens with the date 1801, suggesting both a new beginning and a diary entry. The narrator, Mr Lockwood, is visiting Yorkshire and is the new tenant of Thrushcross Grange. His landlord, who lives at Wuthering Heights, is Heathcliff, described by Lockwood as 'a dark-skinned gipsy in aspect, in dress and manners a gentleman' (p. 5). We are offered a description of the threshold of Wuthering Heights, bearing the date 1500 and the name Hareton Earnshaw, but the history of the property is postponed as Lockwood is intimidated by the surliness of his landlord. In spite of a hostile welcome and an evident lack of desire on Heathcliff's part for the visit to be repeated, Lockwood nevertheless closes the chapter with a vow to return the following day.

The first three chapters detail Lockwood's relationship with his landlord, Heathcliff, and his experience of a sequence of vivid and inexplicable dreams in Heathcliff's home, Wuthering Heights. The narrative then passes to Nelly Dean, who takes us back in time to Heathcliff's arrival at the Heights as a child.

CHILDHOOD

Catherine and Heathcliff grow up as siblings, after Heathcliff is introduced into the Earnshaw household by Catherine's father as a foundling and given the name of a dead son. Their relationship is intense and exclusive: '[Catherine] was much too fond of Heathcliff. The greatest punishment we could invent for her was to keep her separate from him' (p. 42). When their father dies, Catherine's brother Hindley returns to Wuthering Heights with a wife, Frances, and becomes the master of the house. Hindley's wish to sever the intimacy between Catherine and Heathcliff is given unexpected opportunity when Catherine spends five weeks at the neighbouring house, Thrushcross Grange, following a foot injury caused by the owners' guard dog. Catherine returns to the Heights transformed into a lady, having made friends with the children of the Grange – Edgar and Isabella. While Catherine has been away, Hindley has systematically degraded Heathcliff, refusing him education and insisting that he work as a labourer on the grounds. Hindley and Frances have a son, Hareton, shortly after which Frances dies.

MARRIAGE

Following Catherine's decision to marry Edgar, Heathcliff disappears for three years, and Catherine moves to Thrushcross Grange. Her marriage to Edgar is described as affectionate, if subdued. In other words it conforms to the conventions of marriage in the nineteenth century. It is a marriage typified by a kind of quiet friendliness, and as such it is utterly at odds with what we have previously seen of Catherine's character.

Nelly Dean, the housekeeper, moves with Catherine from the Heights. When Heathcliff returns he is quite transformed into an imposing and compelling figure of a man. He enraptures Catherine, and captivates Isabella, much to the annoyance of Edgar.

HEATHCLIFF AND ISABELLA

Heathcliff stays at Wuthering Heights, with his former enemy Hindley, whom he engages in gambling and drinking. In spite of multiple warnings, Isabella falls in love with Heathcliff, who sees that she might well be his route to seeking revenge upon Edgar for depriving him of Catherine.

Edgar and Heathcliff argue violently, precipitating illness in Catherine. Heathcliff courts Isabella. Isabella and Heathcliff elope and Edgar disowns his sister.

For two months Edgar nurses Catherine, and there is no word from Isabella or Heathcliff. Then a letter from Isabella to Nelly Dean reveals that they are back at Wuthering Heights, and that the marriage is desperately unhappy. She begs Nelly to visit her. Nelly goes to visit her at the Heights. Heathcliff makes a passionate declaration of his love for Catherine, and an equally powerful vilification of Isabella. Nelly berates him for his treatment of Isabella, but in the end relents and carries a letter from him to deliver to Catherine. This marks the end of the first volume.

THE NEXT GENERATION

Volume II commences with a visit from Heathcliff to Catherine. He sees that her death is both imminent and inevitable. She dies that evening, giving birth prematurely to a daughter, Cathy.

Isabella flees Heathcliff and her oppressive marriage, for the South of England, where a few months later she gives birth to a son, Linton Heathcliff. At about this time Hindley dies, leaving Heathcliff alone at the Heights with Hareton, whom Heathcliff treats as badly as Hindley had treated him. When Isabella dies, Linton, now twelve and a sickly, effeminate child, returns to Thrushcross Grange with Edgar. Heathcliff sends for him and he returns to Wuthering Heights to live with his father.

Young Cathy lives in cherished seclusion at Thrushcross Grange. Her cousin's existence at the Heights is kept from her. On her sixteenth birthday, however, she meets Heathcliff and Hareton by chance on the moors and returns with them to Wuthering Heights where she is astonished to see Linton.

Heathcliff plans that Cathy and Linton should marry, for then he can gain control of both houses. Linton is peevishly sick, but Cathy's generosity commits her to making his life happier, a generosity which Heathcliff exploits fully.

Cathy is forbidden by Edgar to return to the Heights, but contrives to write to Linton instead. Eventually, she gets the opportunity to pay him visits undetected by either Edgar or Nelly Dean.

Heathcliff's plan that the two cousins should marry is under time pressure, because of Linton's ill health. Heathcliff's obsession with revenge drives him to tyranny. Eventually he forces a marriage between the two, since he is unable to manipulate events in any other way.

Edgar dies, and Thrushcross Grange passes to Linton as the only son of Isabella, rather than to Cathy, the daughter of Edgar. When Linton dies soon afterwards, Heathcliff claims inheritance of Thrushcross Grange, since Cathy is now his daughter-in-law. Thus cruelly dispossessed, Cathy lives in miserable seclusion at the Heights. This brings us to the point at which Lockwood arrives as tenant of Thrushcross Grange, and introduces himself into the household.

The final three chapters of the second volume, mirroring the first three of the first, restore the narrative to Lockwood, who returns to the Heights a year later, to find that Heathcliff has died and Cathy and Hareton are enjoying a blissful courtship prior to their impending marriage.

CONTEXT **A04**

Brontë's understanding of the intricacies of nineteenth-century property law is evident from the complex plot structure. In the nineteenth century there was a fundamental difference between the law of the land (property) and that of goods and money (personal property). The law of the land was such that males were preferred to females. Males inherited according to seniority of birth. Females, if they were to inherit, did so equally.

CHECK THE BOOK **A03**

In his 1926 essay *The Structure of 'Wuthering Heights'*, C. P. Sanger makes a detailed examination of the legal aspects of *Wuthering Heights* and identifies the complex route that Heathcliff makes to take possession of both the Heights and Thrushcross Grange.

VOLUME I, CHAPTER I

SUMMARY

- It is the year 1801. While staying in Yorkshire, Mr Lockwood pays his landlord, Heathcliff, a somewhat unwelcome visit in order to introduce himself.
- We are introduced to Lockwood, Heathcliff, Heathcliff's servant Joseph and a female servant.
- The property Wuthering Heights is described.

ANALYSIS

CONTEXT A04

'I never told my love' is a reference to Shakespeare's *Twelfth Night*, Act II, Scene 4, lines 114–16, establishing Lockwood as an educated narrator.

STUDY FOCUS: THE NARRATORS A02

The chapter opens with Lockwood, an outsider, coming into a world which he finds hostile and unnerving. Recounting his visit to Wuthering Heights, and his meeting with Heathcliff, Lockwood is established as an unreliable and vain **narrator**: 'I felt interested in a man who seemed more exaggeratedly reserved than myself' (p. 3).

TIME

As some critics, most notably C. P. Sanger, have noted, Brontë pays careful attention to time. Although the exact date is only mentioned three times, there are many indications of the time, such as seasonal references and ages of characters, which alert us to the complex time shifts in this novel. That chronological exactitude is of primary importance is established at the very beginning, since the first word of the novel is in fact the date, 1801. This date, which is suggestive of a diary entry, grounds the fiction in a specific historical moment. It sets up our expectations for the novel as a story set in reality, expectations which are then radically challenged as the **narrative** progresses, and the story is passed from Lockwood to Nelly Dean (see below).

The critic Q. D. Leavis links the importance of time in the novel to its social context. She remarks in her essay 'A Fresh Approach to *Wuthering Heights*': 'The point about dating this novel as ending in 1801 (instead of its being contemporary with the Brontës' own lives) … is to fix its happenings at a time when the old rough farming culture based on a naturally patriarchal family life, was to be challenged, tamed and routed by social and cultural changes' (reprinted in Patsy Stoneman (ed.), *Wuthering Heights: Contemporary Critical Essays*, 1993, p. 31). In other words, by setting the story very clearly in the past Brontë could demonstrate the point at which a whole way of life was to change, with the traditional values of the farming lifestyle challenged by ideas about progress, culture and civilisation.

GLOSSARY

4 **penetralium** the innermost parts or recesses of the building, most especially a temple. This use of a highly specialised Latinate term is indicative of Lockwood's education and sophistication

6 **gnarl** snarl

STUDY FOCUS: THE NARRATIVE A02

Employing the double narratives of Lockwood and Nelly (Nelly's narrative commences part way through the fourth chapter) was a highly original technique, permitting Brontë to comment upon the nature of narratorial perspective. This technique also alerts us to the fact that different kinds of knowledge, and different kinds of world view, will compete with each other for precedence in this novel. Lockwood's narrative is more self-consciously literary, written almost as a diary entry; Nelly's is more intimate and more dramatic in tone, drawing us in to the world of the novel. Nelly's is a narrative of original immediacy, contrasted with Lockwood's complex, Latinate and florid style, given to many sub-clauses and adjectives. Simply put, Nelly's is an oral, storytelling narrative, and Lockwood's is literary, suggestive of a written account. Within these narrative frameworks we will find other more condensed narratives such as Catherine's diary.

VOLUME I, CHAPTER II

SUMMARY

- Lockwood repeats his visit to the Heights and meets Hareton and Cathy Heathcliff.
- Lockwood mistakes a heap of dead rabbits for a cushion full of cats, revealing him as an unreliable observer, who sees only what he expects to see.
- He also antagonises Hareton by trying to guess at the family relationships, and in the end Heathcliff is obliged to explain that both his wife and his son are dead and that Cathy is his daughter-in-law.
- Because of a blizzard, Lockwood is forced to spend the night as a guest at the Heights.

ANALYSIS

LOCKWOOD THE OUTSIDER

This chapter clearly conveys the structural and social differences between Lockwood's expectations and the conventions he comes into contact with in Yorkshire. His desire to dine at five, for example, reflects a non-labouring lifestyle. Through the character of Joseph, Brontë provides a convincing rendition of Yorkshire dialect, which again serves to position Lockwood as an outsider, unable to comprehend the ordinary **discourse** of the region. He is equipped with only his conventional notions of the world, and his pitiful misreading of the domestic situation stands as a warning against the assumption that a conventional understanding, or what seems like common sense, will be a reliable guide to a situation.

REVISION FOCUS: TASK 1 `A02`

How far do you agree with the following statements?

- Lockwood is an unreliable narrator.
- Wuthering Heights and Thrushcross Grange represent two completely different ways of seeing the world.

Write opening paragraphs for essays based on these discussion points. Set out your arguments clearly.

KEY QUOTATIONS: VOLUME I, CHAPTER II `A01`

Key quotation 1: 'A sorrowful sight I saw; dark night coming down prematurely, and sky and hills mingled into one bitter whirl of wind and suffocating snow.

"I don't think it possible for me to get home now without a guide."' (p. 14)

Possible interpretation:

- Brontë uses external descriptions here to indicate an internal state: Lockwood feels himself to be at the mercy of potentially threatening conditions, and cannot see his way to what is familiar territory.

Key quotation 2: '"Then I hope his ghost will haunt you; and I hope Mr Heathcliff will never get another tenant, till the Grange is a ruin!" [Cathy] answered sharply.' (p. 17)

Possible interpretation:

- This is the first mention of the supernatural as a guiding moral force in this novel.

CHECK THE BOOK `A03`

Note another reference to Shakespeare on p. 17 – *King Lear*, Act II, Scene 4, lines 279–82. This reference to *King Lear* primarily serves to confirm Lockwood as educated (but not discerning). It might also be read as indicative of the themes of madness and rationality, inheritance and family power struggles, which are integral to this novel.

GLOSSARY

9 **Whet are ye for?** What do you want?
9 **i't'fowld** in the field
10 **ut'laithe** in the barn
10 **flaysome** fearful
12 **discussed** ate
15 **un war** and worse
15 **a nowt** a nothing, useless
15 **aght** out
17 **shoo** she
18 **agait** afoot
18 **Wisht!** Hush!

VOLUME I, CHAPTER III

SUMMARY

● Zillah, the housekeeper at Wuthering Heights, shows Lockwood to a room at the top of the house which, she confides, is both secret and forbidden.

● The room is covered with the name 'Catherine' in different forms: Catherine Earnshaw, Catherine Linton, Catherine Heathcliff.

● Lockwood has two dreams, in the second of which he encounters the ghost of Catherine.

● Lockwood cries out to Catherine's ghost, waking Heathcliff and causing him great distress.

● The next morning Heathcliff guides Lockwood back to the Grange, to which he returns disorientated and 'feeble as a kitten' (p. 32).

ANALYSIS

DREAMS

This is a chapter which has received much critical attention. Containing Lockwood's two dreams, it clearly lends itself to a **psychoanalytic** reading, a reading which treats the novel itself like a dream, a fiction of the mind, which must be interpreted before its meaning can be clearly understood. As Philip K. Wion points out in his psychoanalytic reading of the novel ('The Absent Mother in Emily Brontë's *Wuthering Heights*', 1985), dreams and hallucinations are forms of seeing in which the boundaries between the self and the world are broken down, since in dreams the dreamer is often both an observer and a participant. The names inscribed upon the windowsill can be linked to the same idea, as they show Catherine's awareness of the conflicting elements of her own identity. The order they appear in marks her journey from child – Catherine Earnshaw; through her passionate years with Heathcliff – Catherine Heathcliff; to adulthood and marriage – Catherine Linton.

Dreams in this novel are both visionary, in that they help us to see beyond actual events, and mysterious. They are treated with respect and fear, for they show us an unpredictable and disturbing world. For Brontë, dreams offered a way of representing things which were way beyond the limits of literary decorum for the nineteenth-century novel. Almost all the dreams in this novel deal with taboo subjects: death, religion, love versus passion. Small wonder, then, that it received such puzzled and outraged reviews upon first publication.

REPETITION AND MIRRORING

Frank Kermode (1987) reads the repetitions of Catherine's names in a different way – as evidence of the very isolated nature of the society, and also as essential to the structure of the story:

you see the point of the order of the scribbled names, as Lockwood gives them: Catherine Earnshaw, Catherine Heathcliff, Catherine Linton. Read from left to right they recapitulate the late Catherine Earnshaw's story; read from right to left, the story of her daughter, Catherine Linton. The names Catherine and Earnshaw begin and end the narrative … this is an account of the movement of the book: away from Earnshaw and back, like the movement of the house itself. And all the movements must be through Heathcliff. (p. 139)

> **GRADE BOOSTER** **A02**
>
> There are many layers and repetitions in this novel. Examiners will be impressed if you use the literary term '**palimpsest**' to describe all the different layers of meaning. Remember, too, that in an essay requiring you to analyse repetition it is particularly important that you set out your argument.

A **structuralist** reading of the chapter would focus upon the complex, interlocking structure of this text: what has been called its 'Chinese-box' structure by C. P. Sanger (*The Structure of 'Wuthering Heights'*, 1926). Mirroring the text-within-a-text structure of the novel, the bedroom to which Lockwood is shown contains within it a cleverly designed panelled structure which serves as both bed and little closet. We have the bedroom within the bedroom, the texts within the text which are themselves palimpsests, written over with Catherine's diary entries; the dreams, which contain sleepiness within sleeping, texts within texts again, and secrets within secrets.

STUDY FOCUS: *WUTHERING HEIGHTS* AS PARABLE   A03

J. Hillis Miller's influential **deconstructive** reading of the chapter (*Fiction and Repetition*, 1982) discusses the palimpsestic nature of the texts, in which each text can be seen as a commentary upon a previous one. His reading follows this path: Catherine's diary is described by Lockwood as a commentary, written in the margins of Branderham's sermon. That sermon is itself a commentary upon a text of the New Testament in which Jesus enjoins his followers to forgive seventy times seven. The first of the seventy-first is therefore to be understood as the unpardonable sin. The story from the Bible is Jesus's interpretation of the nature of forgiveness, and includes a reading of several phrases from the Old Testament. Jesus's interpretation is characteristically accompanied by a **parable**. A parable is a story which explains or illustrates an abstract concept.

Wuthering Heights can be read as a parable, then, in that it is Lockwood's narration of a story which is adjacent to or in the margins of the mysterious events which he is trying to understand. Miller's reading focuses attention on the role of margins in this novel; he comments upon the difficulty of identifying the exact beginning of the novel, prefaced as it is by so many introductions. Lockwood's dreams can be seen as an example of precisely this difficulty of locating an exact beginning or meaning.

REVISION FOCUS: TASK 2   A02

Consider the importance of the following in *Wuthering Heights*:

● Repetition and the 'Chinese box' structure

● Dreams and the supernatural

Write opening paragraphs for essays based on these discussion points. Set out your arguments clearly.

GLOSSARY

21	**nut o'ered**	not over
21	**lugs**	ears
21	**laiking**	playing
21	**scroop**	the spine of a book
21	**pawsed his fit**	kicked his feet
21	**laced**	thrashed
29	**Grimalkin**	name of a cat, as for example the witches' cat Greymalkin, in *Macbeth*

VOLUME I, CHAPTER IV

SUMMARY

- While recovering from his trip to the Heights, Lockwood engages his housekeeper, Nelly Dean, to tell him the story of the inhabitants of Wuthering Heights.
- We learn that Cathy Heathcliff is the last of the Lintons, just as Hareton is the last of the Earnshaws.
- Nelly hints that Heathcliff has cheated Hareton out of his rightful inheritance.
- Nelly Dean takes over the narration at this point and we learn something of Heathcliff's history: how he was rescued from the port of Liverpool by Mr Earnshaw, his growing friendship with Catherine and his feud with her brother Hindley.
- Two years later Mrs Earnshaw dies and the children all fall sick with the measles. This endears Heathcliff to Nelly Dean, as he is least complaining, unlike Hindley and Catherine.
- The chapter closes with the incident of the two colts. Heathcliff takes the best and, when his falls lame, takes Hindley's.

ANALYSIS

HEATHCLIFF'S ARRIVAL

From the moment he arrives, Heathcliff occupies a conflicting and contradictory position in the household, and in the story. He is both a ghostly substitute for a dead elder son and 'a wicked boy' (p. 50) 'possessed of something diabolical' (p. 66). He is also quite beyond the formal societal constraints of the family and the Church, having but one name that serves him for both purposes.

Hindley's behaviour towards Heathcliff is brutish and violent. Heathcliff, once he gets his way, is self-contained and apparently unvindictive, though tantalisingly Nelly confides that in this assessment she was 'deceived, completely' (p. 40). Read in conjunction with the qualities he shows in illness, Heathcliff's attitude here can be seen as revealing of his unwavering ambition and determination to achieve his heart's desire. He sees no point in wasting emotional energy, and he is oblivious to the emotional life of others.

The arrival of Heathcliff at the Heights has been the focus of much critical attention. In *The Madwoman in the Attic: The Woman Writer and the Nineteenth-Century Literary Imagination* (1979), Sandra Gilbert and Susan Gubar read this arrival in terms of gender roles, paying attention to the whip as a symbol of masculinity, which Catherine has requested and which is lost only to be replaced by Heathcliff.

In *Myths of Power: A Marxist Study of the Brontës* (1992), a **Marxist** reading of the novel, Terry Eagleton sees Heathcliff's presence at the Heights as both radical and random. Because Heathcliff's origins are so obscure, and because his family relationships place him outside the conventional social structure of the family, he is available to be loved or hated for himself. His lack of social status or clear social role, coupled with Mr Earnshaw's favouritism, disrupts any certainty about rightful inheritance, causing Hindley to feel, rightly, threatened, and Catherine, equally rightly, strengthened.

GRADE BOOSTER **A02**

Take note of key points you can analyse for AO2. The description of Lockwood as a kitten serves to identify him as similar to Edgar, who is described as a cat in Chapter VIII. Their similarities extend to their refined and fastidious natures, their education and their social status.

CRITICAL VIEWPOINT **A03**

It can be argued that Heathcliff's stoicism and patience in illness, which here are the qualities that endear him to Nelly, are precisely the qualities that he draws on later as he exacts his revenge on those around him.

A NEW NARRATOR

The most significant aspect of this chapter is the change of **narrator** from Lockwood, whom we have come to see as unreliable, to Nelly Dean, who has the advantage of having lived with the main protagonists and who is thus able to explain their characters to Lockwood.

This doubling of narrator reminds us, as J. Hillis Miller points out, not to be too overconfident as readers. The switch from Lockwood to Nelly is immediately unsettling and removes our certainty that the narrator's voice is neutral or trustworthy. This device of an external masculine **narrative** framing and giving legitimacy to an internal feminine narrative was also used by Anne Brontë in *The Tenant of Wildfell Hall*. It can be seen in relation to Emily Brontë's use of the masculine-sounding pseudonym 'Ellis Bell' to legitimate her own novel.

STUDY FOCUS: DOMESTIC POWER   A04

It is important to note that when Nelly Dean takes up the narration we are presented with a narrative whose subject and interest consist entirely of domestic action and adventure. The structure of power is an important theme for Brontë, and she treats it in a very complex way, revealing its contradictory yet never confused relationships. The prevailing wisdom about power in the nineteenth century was that men had it and women didn't. If women had any power at all, it was confined to the home. Brontë's characters, however, disrupt these ideas about power, who it belongs to and how they use it. While she is clearly aware of and understands the impact of property laws upon women's wealth and influence, Brontë suggests that we should not underestimate the domestic power that women are sometimes able to operate. At the end of the novel it is her female characters who have the upper hand: Cathy, bathed in glowing moonlight and the warmth from the fire, is teaching a willingly submissive Hareton his letters; similarly, Nelly is able to silence Joseph, and expertly manages the financial affairs of both properties.

To get the best grades at AS and A2 you need to show an excellent understanding of the contexts that lie behind the text. The relationship between the different kinds of power is elegantly exemplified in the relationship between the two narrators. Lockwood, although he is woefully incapable of reading the **discourse** of his new environment and utterly incompetent at understanding the writing on the sill, is nevertheless able as a man, and as Heathcliff's tenant, to prevail upon Nelly Dean to sit and tell him stories way beyond her working hours. Nelly, on the other hand, reader of all the books in the library and recipient of important letters, controls a great deal of the action of the novel through her choices about what to do with such privileged information.

CRITICAL VIEWPOINT A03

Nelly's description of the family tree curiously identifies Hareton as 'the late Mrs Linton's nephew' (p. 34) rather than the late Mr Earnshaw's son which subtly locates him in the house on which his name does not appear This, it could be argued, prefigures the plotline.

KEY QUOTATION: VOLUME I, CHAPTER IV   A01

Key quotation: '"you must e'en take [Heathcliff] as a gift of God; though it's as dark almost as if it came from the devil"' (p. 36)

Possible interpretations:

- The link between Heathcliff and the devil adds a **Gothic** element to the novel.
- From these first words Heathcliff is associated with the idea of a battle between Heaven and Hell.
- There is a sense of foreboding about Heathcliff's arrival – Mr Earnshaw's words can be read as a warning that the child must be treated with respect.

GLOSSARY

33 **strike my colours** a naval term meaning to show the flag for surrender

35 **dunnock** sparrow

36 **flighted** frightened

VOLUME I, CHAPTER V

SUMMARY

- Nelly Dean recounts how the family relationships develop in divisive ways as Mr Earnshaw's health fails.
- Hindley continues to bully Heathcliff and humiliate him. Hindley is eventually sent away to college on the advice of the curate who is offering the family private tuition. Mr Earnshaw agrees reluctantly as he does not believe that Hindley will benefit from college.
- We are given our first sustained description of Catherine.
- Mr Earnshaw dies quietly one October evening. Both Catherine and Heathcliff are utterly distraught, and comfort each other.

ANALYSIS

FAMILY RELATIONSHIPS

The focus of this chapter is Catherine's relationships with her father and Heathcliff, of whom, Nelly suggests, Catherine is much too fond. However, the description of Catherine as deliberately infuriating and rebellious, and indeed of Heathcliff as some sort of devilish progeny, is counterbalanced by their response to her father's death, which Nelly describes as both anguished and innocent. Contradiction is seen to be an integral part of the way in which people relate to each other. It is this acknowledgement of internal contradiction that has led critics to see the novel as morally ambivalent. It is also worth noting that at this early point in the novel Brontë is already pitting an unmediated spiritual belief against the stern religious dogma of Joseph. When Catherine and Heathcliff comfort each other at Mr Earnshaw's death, Nelly Dean comments: 'no parson in the world ever pictured Heaven so beautifully as they did, in their innocent talk'(p. 44).

As Mr Earnshaw's health begins to fail, his favouritism of Heathcliff becomes even more pronounced. Hindley continues to scorn Heathcliff, which enrages his weakening father. Nelly's hope that Hindley's removal would restore some peace to the household is undermined by a crucial unspoken acknowledgement. It seems that the source of the tension is Heathcliff: 'It hurt me to think the master should be made uncomfortable by his own good deed' (p. 41).

GRADE BOOSTER A02

Be prepared for challenging questions. You may be asked about the importance of childhood in this novel, or to choose two of the minor characters and discuss their relevance to the main themes of the novel.

STUDY FOCUS: A ROMANTIC VISION OF CHILDHOOD A04

In this chapter Brontë describes Catherine as wild and wicked, but also, in her first description of her, shows her as beautiful, lively and wayward, but with a good heart. The vision of childhood that Brontë portrays is irrepressibly **Romantic**: the children are full of the authority of their own natural vitality. The passage has been read as an example of the Romantic theme of the child in conflict with society. If we accept such a reading, it is noteworthy that Brontë permits Catherine the last word: 'Why cannot you always be a good man, father?' (p. 43).

KEY QUOTATIONS: VOLUME I, CHAPTER V   A01

Key quotation 1:

The first description of Catherine shows her as beautiful, lively and wayward, but with a good heart:

'A wild, wick slip she was – but, she had the bonniest eye, and the sweetest smile, and the lightest foot in the parish; and after all, I believe she meant no harm' (p. 42).

Possible interpretations:

- The 'wild, wick slip' demonstrates Catherine's vitality, full of life in contrast to her dying father, and in contrast to the expectations of genteel girlhood.
- The descriptions of Catherine show her as spontaneous and impulsive, which sets up our expectations of her character as a Romantic heroine later in the novel.

Key quotation 2:

'His [Mr Earnshaw's] peevish reproofs wakened in her a naughty delight to provoke him; she was never so happy as when we were all scolding her at once, and she defying us with her bold, saucy look, and her ready words; turning Joseph's religious curses into ridicule …'(p. 43).

Possible interpretations:

- This quotation shows Catherine to be a selfish and unsympathetic character and an unlikely heroine.
- Catherine has no respect for authority, neither for her father, her nurse, nor for Joseph's religious authority.

Key quotation 3:

'The poor thing discovered her loss directly – she screamed out –

"Oh he's dead, Heathcliff! He's dead!"

And they both set up a heart-breaking cry.

I joined my wail to theirs, loud and bitter; but Joseph asked what we could be thinking of to roar in that way over a saint in Heaven.' (p. 44)

Possible interpretations:

- The children's unrestrained grief at the death of their father is in direct contrast to Joseph's gruff insistence on dogma. This conveys their willingness to live a life of passion rather than a life filtered through the context of religious propriety.
- Brontë devotes very little physical description to Joseph. Almost all we know of him comes through his dialogue, which is often anchored in both biblical references and superstition.

CHECK THE BOOK   A04

Juliet Barker's biography of the Brontës (1994) has some particularly insightful passages about death and how important it was in the poetry of Emily Brontë and the novels of both Emily and Anne.

VOLUME I, CHAPTER VI

SUMMARY

- Following the death of his father, Hindley returns as the master of the Heights, with a wife, Frances, who is described as poor, ill and silly.
- As the new master, Hindley finds vent for all his old hatred of Heathcliff. He denies him an education, insists that he should labour out of doors and makes him live with the servants.
- Despite Hindley's endeavours, Catherine and Heathcliff remain inseparable and wild.
- We have our first introduction to Edgar and Isabella Linton, who live at the neighbouring house, Thrushcross Grange.
- Catherine is hurt on one of her escapades with Heathcliff, and is obliged to remain at Thrushcross Grange until she is considered well enough to return to the Heights.

ANALYSIS

HEAVEN AND HELL

Critics have often focused upon the structural differences between Thrushcross Grange and Wuthering Heights. The splendid, cultivated and civilised atmosphere at the Grange is compared with the rough indiscipline of the Heights. Most famously, David Cecil (*Victorian Novelists: Essays in Revaluation*, 1935) has argued that the differences between the Heights and the Grange can be thought of as corresponding to a **metaphysical** opposition between storm and calm. And yet, as Gilbert and Gubar (*The Madwoman in the Attic: The Woman Writer and the Nineteenth-Century Literary Imagination*, 1979) point out, the violence which one might naturally associate with the Heights is no less present at the Grange. They argue that Catherine, for example, does not so much willingly enter the world of Thrushcross Grange, but rather is seized by it. Indeed, as Terry Eagleton (1992) points out, the more property one has, the more ferociously one needs to protect it (see **Violence**, below).

In their reading of the novel in Chapter 8 of *The Madwoman in the Attic*, the **feminist** critics Sandra Gilbert and Susan Gubar see *Wuthering Heights* as a 'Bible of Hell' in that it is a novel which privileges the natural over the cultural, the freedom of anarchy over domestic life and repressed feelings. The domain of Wuthering Heights is certainly anarchic judged by conventional standards. Indeed, in Chapter II we are encouraged by Lockwood to read it as hellish with his remarks upon the 'dismal spiritual atmosphere' (p. 14) and Heathcliff's 'almost diabolical' (p. 13) smile. But it can also be read as representing another challenge to convention in that it is an ungovernable social space, in other words one without authority. As such, it is a space in which both Catherine and Heathcliff can exercise power. In almost any other environment in the nineteenth century this power would be denied to them, she being female and he being illegitimate.

VIOLENCE

Violence characterises life at Wuthering Heights, where the children are often beaten, in apparent contrast to the 'petted' (p. 48) lives of the children at Thrushcross Grange. So it is worth paying attention to the fact that Thrushcross Grange is the site of the first real act of aggression between the two houses. As Catherine and Heathcliff peep in through the windows of the Grange, they are noticed and set upon by guard dogs and Catherine is caught by the ankle and savaged. Thus she is unable to return to the Heights with Heathcliff.

Captured, in fairy-tale manner, by the 'civilised' world of Thrushcross Grange, Catherine yields to what she understands to be her destiny, even as she sees that this life is quite opposite to her character. Later, anguished and despairing, she resists her life with Edgar Linton and finds her only way out of it by death. Literally she 'catches her death' by throwing open the window in Chapter XII. This act of opening the window can be read as rupturing the fortifications of the civilised life to let in the fresh air of the natural, an act of such symbolic violence that it can only result in death.

STUDY FOCUS: A MIRROR IMAGE   A02

Heathcliff admires the comparative luxury of the Grange and acknowledges its beauty. He even compares it to a kind of heaven, but he remains entirely devoted to the freedom of his life with Catherine, and cannot comprehend the selfishness of the spoiled children: 'When would you catch me wishing to have what Catherine wanted?' (p. 48).

This question is **rhetorical**. What Heathcliff cannot imagine is quarrelling with Catherine over something she wants, since their needs and desires are exactly matched. What appalls him are the opposing, individual, selfish needs of the Linton children. The image of the two civilised children inside the beautiful room, and the two wild children outside, both pairs a boy and girl of similar ages, can be read as though the glass of the window is a kind of mirror. However, this is a mirror which reflects opposition, desire and otherness. It has thus provided rich material for both **structuralist** and **psychoanalytic** readings.

HEATHCLIFF'S LANGUAGE

This chapter gives the child Heathcliff his first major speech, and it is worth noting how his language differs from that of the other characters. He is expressive and emotional, and this encourages us to identify with his unmediated, unguarded response. His speech is more literary than Ellen's and less artificial than Lockwood's. He tends to speak in extreme and vibrant terms. Expressing his scorn for Edgar Linton's cowardice and weak politeness, he says:

> I'd not exchange, for a thousand lives, my condition here, for Edgar Linton's at Thrushcross Grange – not if I might have the privilege of flinging Joseph off the highest gable, and painting the house-front with Hindley's blood! (p. 49)

Note that in aligning ourselves with Heathcliff as the vital and wronged party here we are already accepting and endorsing the violence that is to characterise his behaviour as the novel progresses. Heathcliff's threat to paint the house with Hindley's blood and fling Joseph off the gable top is an empty one at this point, but it nevertheless presages what is to come. It can also be read as representing a real desire to topple conventional religious authority in favour of a more 'natural' spirituality and to sever the authority of Hindley's bloodline, making Wuthering Heights his own.

CONTEXT   A04

This depiction of domestic violence is entirely in conflict with the conventional Victorian notion of the home as the ideal refuge from the harshness of the outside world.

CRITICAL VIEWPOINT   A03

As Alexander and Smith note in *The Oxford Companion to the Brontës* (2006), the 'family knew the works of Shakespeare almost as well as they did the Bible'. The connection between blood and revenge is central to both this novel and *Macbeth*.

GLOSSARY

46 **foreigners** strangers

50 **Lascar** east-Indian seaman

51 **negus** hot toddy made of wine and water

VOLUME I, CHAPTER VII

SUMMARY

- Catherine returns from her five-week stay at Thrushcross Grange, transformed into a lady.
- Heathcliff has been systematically debased by Hindley during this time.
- The Linton children have been invited to Wuthering Heights the next day in order to thank them for nursing Catherine.
- Heathcliff begs Nelly to make him decent, but Hindley and Edgar Linton both try to humiliate Heathcliff, who retaliates violently.
- Heathcliff is dismissed and Catherine, apparently unfeelingly, continues to have tea with her new friends.
- Eventually she creeps away from the tea party to be with Heathcliff, and Heathcliff plots his revenge on Hindley.
- The end of this chapter reminds us that this is a story being related to Lockwood by Nelly Dean.

ANALYSIS

CRITICAL VIEWPOINT A03

As Ruth Robbins clarifies in *Literary Feminisms* (2000): 'Thrushcross Grange, across the moor, home of the Linton family, represents the standards of patriarchal culture which will be triumphant at the end of the story, but which the novel itself, through its sympathies for Cathy and Heathcliff, implicitly attacks' (p. 92).

TWO DIFFERENT WORLDS

This chapter is the first to demonstrate explicitly the differences between the two houses, Thrushcross Grange and Wuthering Heights – differences which represent the central oppositions of the novel. Catherine stays at Thrushcross Grange for five weeks until she is deemed healthy, both in body and in manners. She returns to the Heights a very 'dignified person' (p. 53), dressed in fine clothes and quite transformed from the person she has been. We can see that Thrushcross Grange therefore symbolises civilisation and status. Heathcliff, by contrast, is forbiddingly unkempt, but Catherine's love of him is undiminished and she embraces him immediately.

BOUNDARIES AND BARRIERS

Once again, critical attention might be paid to the boundaries and barriers in this chapter. Just as the window separated the Wuthering Heights children from the Lintons in the last chapter, here too a material object separates Catherine from Heathcliff. The fine dress she wears to return to the Heights represents a very real boundary between the old friends: it must be sacrificed (smudged, crumpled) if the two of them are to be as close as they were before. It is valuable simultaneously for economic reasons (its cost), for social ones (the respect it earns Catherine), and because of its artificial beauty. These same categories will consistently come between Catherine and Heathcliff: he is right to recognise the dress and what it represents as a threat to his happiness. The dress thus signifies the artifice of civilisation which Catherine must put on and which will alienate her from Heathcliff, with devastating consequences.

The bed to which Heathcliff retires hurt is precisely the bed which had housed Lockwood's disturbing dreams in the third chapter. Here, too, its panels and windows operate to form a series of boundaries behind which secrets can be concealed.

CHECK THE BOOK A03

Michael Macovski's essay 'Voicing a Silent History: *Wuthering Heights* as Dialogic Text' (1987; reprinted in Patsy Stoneman (ed.), *Wuthering Heights: Contemporary Critical Essays*, 1993) offers an intriguing reading of the novel as a series of stories.

NELLY AND LOCKWOOD

Finally, Nelly Dean interrupts her **narrative** to focus upon Lockwood, who requires her to continue her story even though it is late in the day. Lockwood comments on the class and type of people he has encountered in the region, and Nelly calls his hasty judgements and patronising attitude to our attention by remarking that he 'could not open a book in this library that [she had] not looked into' (p. 63). Lockwood's failure to read Nelly Dean in any terms other than the conventions of class is further reinforced by his insensitivity to Nelly's hours of sleep and work. She characteristically deflates his pompous speech on the type of people native to the region by drawing attention to both her level of formal education and the lessons learned from the demanding aspects of her life. A **feminist** reading of the novel would consider how Brontë emphasises the power of female discourse with Nelly's account here. Lockwood's inability to contemplate the broader picture is perceived by both Nelly and the reader to be a failure of intellect as much as of experience.

RELIGION AND FREEDOM

This chapter once again offers an interestingly nuanced view of religion. Joseph's surly, isolated religion which sees him retiring in 'private prayer' is pitted against Nelly's conventionally celebratory religion 'singing carols' (p. 55), and then further contrasted with the free-spirited life of the children as Heathcliff, waiting until the rest of the family have departed for church, goes out onto the moors which returns him 'to a better spirit' (p. 56) and determined to be good.

STUDY FOCUS: EMILY BRONTË AND RELIGION A04

Emily Brontë's views on religion might be thought particularly unorthodox for the daughter of a parson. They are indicative of the fact that her father believed in a great many freedoms for his children, not least of which was intellectual freedom. Katherine Frank remarks on Emily Brontë's 'peculiar faith' in her book *Emily Brontë: A Chainless Soul* (1990). She draws on examples from Emily Brontë's poetry to show that Emily was not a Christian in the conventional sense of the term.

REVISION FOCUS: TASK 3 A04

- Consider the importance of religion for this novel.
- Discuss the relationship between class and empathy in *Wuthering Heights*.

Write an opening paragraph for each of these essay titles. Set out your arguments clearly.

Andrea Arnold's film *Wuthering Heights* (2011) casts James Howson as the first black Heathcliff, referencing the novel's citations of Heathcliff as 'a dark-skinned gipsy' (p. 5). The film uses intimate hand-held camera shots to convey a sense of the novel's rough passion and authenticity. The casting of a black actor as Heathcliff has been considered a move that makes the story more about race than it is about class (Xan Brooks, *Guardian* newspaper, September 2011). Like most screen adaptations of the novel, the film only depicts Volume I, ending with Catherine's death.

GLOSSARY

55 **cant** lively

56 **donning** dressing

KEY QUOTATIONS: VOLUME I, CHAPTER VII

Key quotation 1:

'"I'm trying to settle how I shall pay Hindley back. I don't care how long I wait, if I can only do it, at last. I hope he will not die before I do!"

"For shame, Heathcliff!" said I. "It is for God to punish wicked people; we should learn to forgive."

"No, God won't have the satisfaction that I shall," he returned. "I only wish I knew the best way! Let me alone, and I'll plan it out: while I'm thinking of that, I don't feel pain."' (p. 61)

Possible interpretations:

- This emphasis on revenge blocking out physical pain is the first intimation of Heathcliff's character that sets him on the tragic journey from abandoned orphan to loveless tyrant.
- It links Heathcliff's words to the wider theme of good and evil.
- It shows that Heathcliff lives outside religious faith and moral laws.

Key quotation 2:

At the end of the chapter Lockwood remarks to Nelly Dean: '"I could fancy a love for life here almost possible; and I was a fixed unbeliever in any love"' (p. 62).

Possible interpretations:

- This is a revealing speech from Lockwood and shows him yet again in a negative light. For Brontë, love is the supreme redeemer but he describes himself as an 'unbeliever'.
- It reminds us that this is a story within a story, being told between people who have no understanding of each other.
- It also shows that Lockwood has limited grasp of the fierce passions of the central characters.

VOLUME I, CHAPTER VIII

SUMMARY

- In June 1778, Hindley's son Hareton is born.
- Frances Earnshaw dies of consumption and Hindley declines even further into recklessness. Nelly Dean returns to Wuthering Heights to act as nursemaid to the baby.
- The relationship between Catherine and Edgar is developed, and the tension between Edgar and Heathcliff is intensified. Catherine feels torn between Heathcliff and Edgar.
- Catherine displays violent behaviour, pinching and slapping Nelly and boxing Edgar's ears.

ANALYSIS

HEATHCLIFF OR EDGAR?

This chapter explicitly details the central conflict of the novel: the choice that Catherine has to make between Heathcliff and Edgar Linton. The choice is pivotal to all the events in the novel. It has been variously seen as a choice between passion and social status, authenticity and bad faith, sex and sublimation, risk and security, nature and culture, spirituality and economics. However it is framed, the choice is almost always seen as being between two incompatible ways of life. Catherine's attempts throughout the novel to reconcile the two result in her death, suggesting that they really are fatally opposed realities.

TRANSGRESSION

The chapter also demonstrates Catherine's unruly temper. She transgresses the boundaries of good behaviour in cascading levels of violence. Edgar is shocked at Catherine's assualt on Nelly – she pinches her and slaps her face – and the fact that she promptly lies about it. His attempts to intervene only earn him a box on the ears.

This display of violence can also be seen as a metaphor for Catherine's attempts to transcend her internal conflicts, and we can argue that it anticipates the unquietness of her ghost. Nelly's account of Edgar is that he 'wanted spirit in general' (p. 67), in direct contrast to the description of Catherine's 'naughty spirit' (p. 71), and it is possible to read this both literally and in the context of the supernatural in this novel, for in the end Catherine's spirit transcends death and refuses to be quiet.

In her book *The English Novel: Form and Function* (1961), Dorothy Van Ghent draws our attention to the ways in which form supports the thematic structure of the novel. She observes that the aim to cross physical boundaries represents a wish to transcend psychological barriers and a desire to unite the two incompatible kinds of reality. There are several ways in which the form does this. The dual narration which 'frames' the story in different ways points to the theme of boundaries and transgression. The fact that the narration is contradictory and sometimes confusing suggests that truth is not tidily contained in what we perceive as 'natural' or 'normal', but that it has to be striven for. Van Ghent puts forward an interesting argument that by the end of the novel Heathcliff's daughter-in-law, Cathy Heathcliff, does succeed in achieving the domestic romance.

Van Ghent's thesis has been immensely influential, in that searching for consistent symbols and images is now a standard method of reading a text like *Wuthering Heights*.

CONTEXT A04

Hindley's wife exhibits the symptoms of tuberculosis or consumption, the disease which was to claim the lives of both Emily and Anne Brontë within six months of each other in 1848–9.

GRADE BOOSTER A02

You can improve your grade by drawing parallels between a character's external behaviour and their internal state. Catherine's reluctance for Heathcliff and Edgar to meet stems from the feeling that their differences only highlight her own internal conflicts.

GLOSSARY

64 **rush of a lass** slip of a girl

69 **loading lime** a procedure to make the ground more fertile

VOLUME I, CHAPTER IX

SUMMARY

- Heathcliff and Hindley's relationship deteriorates even further. Hindley is abusive and violent to everyone, threatens Nelly with a carving knife and shows no affection for his infant son.

- Catherine makes her choice between Edgar and Heathcliff and chooses Edgar. There is a long discussion on the nature of love between Catherine and Nelly Dean. Catherine makes it clear that she has chosen to marry Edgar for his looks, his wealth and his position. She says it would 'degrade' her to marry Heathcliff, at which Heathcliff, who has been listening unobserved, disappears.

- Catherine is distraught and goes to search for him on the moors, as a consequence of which she catches a fever and goes once more to recuperate at the Grange.

- Three years later, when Edgar is master of the Grange, he marries Catherine. Heathcliff is absent all this time.

- Nelly reluctantly leaves Hareton and goes with Catherine to live at the Grange.

ANALYSIS

LOVE AND MARRIAGE

On one level this novel can be read as the supreme celebration of a love story, describing a love which defies authority, social convention, even death. Catherine and Heathcliff's love is famously deferred, never consummated and never brought down to the level of trivial day-to-day matters. Theirs is a love which is idealised and magnified, and, in positing such a relationship, the novel both recognises and explicitly appeals to the desire for perfect love.

The central theme of the novel is revealed here as being about the contradictory experiences of love and marriage: Catherine agonises about the practical choice she must make in choosing her future. She recognises that she must choose Edgar, for the implications this has for her and her children's lives; but she refuses to accept that this means forgoing Heathcliff and a life of passion. Catherine describes her thoughts on love through a dream she has had about being unfit to enter heaven (pp. 80–1). **Psychoanalytic critics** have focused their attention on  the dreams in this novel and the ways in which desire is diverted into other, destructive, channels. Other critics, such as **Marxist** and **feminist critics**, have read Catherine's choice between Edgar and Heathcliff in terms of its political implications.

Catherine puts forward her thoughts on marriage as 'a secret' which is making her 'very unhappy' (p. 77). She reveals that she has agreed to marry Edgar Linton for reasons which are, according to Nelly Dean, at best indifferent (because he loves her) and at worst immoral (because they are self-seeking): 'he will be rich, and I shall like to be the greatest woman of the neighbourhood, and I shall be proud of having such a husband' (p. 78).

STUDY FOCUS: A TURNING POINT · A02

Catherine's declaration of love for Heathcliff comes at precisely the moment that she has chosen to marry Edgar, and at the point at which Heathcliff disappears from their lives. It is therefore possible to read this as evidence of how in the novel the consummation of passion is endlessly put off in favour of social convention and restraint. Catherine's uncontrolled love for Heathcliff, which causes her to stay outdoors until she catches the chill which proves deadly to Mr and Mrs Linton, seems incompatible with civilised life, so much so that we could even argue that it kills it. We can see Catherine's vow that anyone who tried to keep her and Heathcliff separate would 'meet the fate of Milo' (p. 81) as a sign that she sees herself trapped between the two worlds.

CONTEXT · A04

Milo was a Greek athlete who attempted to tear an oak in two, but found himself trapped when the cleft closed over his hands. This reference to Catherine being as trapped as an oak is reiterated at the end of the first volume when Heathcliff declares: 'And that insipid, paltry creature attending her from *duty* and *humanity*! From *pity* and *charity*! He might as well plant an oak in a flower-pot, and expect it to thrive, as imagine he can restore her to vigour in the soil of his shallow cares!' (p. 152).

GLOSSARY

77	**grat**	wept
77	**mools**	earth, soil, particularly the soil of a grave
83	**girt**	great, big
83	**eedle**	idle
83	**seeght**	sight
84	**war**	worse
84	**rigs**	ridges
84	**plottered**	blundered
84	**offald**	worthless
86	**bog-hoile**	hole in the marsh
87	**starving**	frozen
87	**gentle and simple**	the upper and lower class
87	**wer**	our

CRITICAL VIEWPOINT · A02

Catherine's earlier speech in Volume I, Chapter IV, about the power of dreams to change lives and to affect reality directly shows that dreams and dreaming is a recurring theme in the novel: 'I've dreamt in my life dreams that have stayed with me ever after, and changed my ideas; they've gone through and through me, like wine through water, and altered the colour of my mind' (p. 79).

EXTENDED COMMENTARY

VOLUME I, CHAPTER IX, PP. 79–81

From 'All seems smooth and easy – where is the obstacle?' to '…as different as a moonbeam from lightning or frost from fire.'

Following the violent incident between Hindley, Heathcliff and Hareton, there comes Catherine's account of Edgar's proposal and her response. She divulges this first in the form of a secret and then of a dream. Nelly fiercely resists the knowledge: '"I won't hear it! I won't hear it!, … I was superstitious about dreams then, and am still"' (p. 80).

The centrality of dreams in this novel permits Brontë to tackle subjects in ways which she simply could not have attempted had she stuck to the limitations of what Julia Swindells (*Victorian Writing and Working Women*, 1985) has called the literary professionalism of the 'Gentleman's Club' in the nineteenth century. Dreams enable Brontë to present ideas about love, religion and identity which would have been thoroughly shocking to the Victorian readership. The novel's violations and reinventions of identity, sexuality and religious taboo are as uncensored as in a dream: they are free from the restrictions of convention. Dreams do not insist upon one story, but often involve many overlapping stories. They often contain contradictions that may well be disturbing, but these contradictions are part of the very structure of dreaming.

Catherine's interpretation of her dream is key to our understanding of her perception of conventional marriage. It is perceived as a kind of paradise, a heaven on earth, but not one to which she feels she can belong:

> I was only going to say that heaven did not seem to be my home; and I broke my heart with weeping to come back to earth; and the angels were so angry that they flung me out, into the middle of the heath on the top of Wuthering Heights; where I woke sobbing for joy. (p. 81)

Notably, in this dream Catherine perceives her choices as moral choices: as choices between good and evil, Heaven and Hell, and she states that she cannot belong in the realm of Heaven but must return to Wuthering Heights, where her joy is to be found.

This dream references the central tension in the novel, between the Christian world of the Lintons, a world in which love is conceived of as Christian charity and social decorum, and the world of Heathcliff, a world of authentic love, which is passionate and unrestrained. But the heavenly world of the Lintons is perceived by Catherine to be a hollow world, a world that cannot be right:

> In whichever place the soul lives – in my soul and in my heart, I'm convinced I'm wrong … I've no more business to marry Edgar Linton than I have to be in heaven. (pp. 80–1)

She is wrong to marry Edgar, because heaven is not a place in which her soul could ever be happy. Nelly hints at this. Later in the novel, Heathcliff insists that these heavenly sentiments of pity and charity would produce a living hell in the absence of real passion.

There is a contradiction, then, in the novel's treatment of the Christian virtue of love. On the one hand it shows Heathcliff as devilish and hardly human. On the other, it suggests that Christian love is self-serving and mean-spirited. In the whole novel, it is only Heathcliff who lays down his life for the love of another. Heathcliff's love is shown as transcendent, and deeper than the love of ordinary men.

Sigmund Freud's *The Interpretation of Dreams*, generally taken to be his major and most original work, can offer a different perspective on this passage. In it Freud investigates dreams, and the phenomenon of dreaming, as the products of a conflict between conscious and unconscious processes of thought. Freud read the strange images and events experienced in dreams as coded **narratives** of the ways in which the unconscious mind is shaped by childhood events. According to his theory, the unconscious mind, repressed by the conscious mind in everyday life, finds expression in the form of dreaming. Applying Freud's theory to this passage, it is interesting to note that Catherine's dream retains its potency precisely because of its repression – she has to physically hold Nelly Dean down to make her listen to it. Furthermore, Catherine begins the account with a denial of it – 'This is nothing' – and a declaration of the conflict between her feelings for Edgar and for Heathcliff.

Catherine's desires, as expressed in her dream, are acknowledged to be immoral, making her unfit for heaven. Using Freudian terms, the dream provides a means of explaining a secret, illicit desire buried in her unconscious mind. This desire is revealed as a desire for the perverse and the unattainable. Because Edgar Linton is incorporated into the structures of allowable desire, he becomes less attractive, shifting attention back to Heathcliff. It seems that, for Brontë, true desire is not directed at an obtainable object, for this would allow the satisfaction of that desire. Instead, desire is most powerful when it is transgressive and when the satisfaction of it is impossible to achieve.

CHECK THE BOOK **A03**

In *The Interpretation of Dreams* (1953), Sigmund Freud offers a detailed investigation of the function of dreams, and the relationship between dreams and thoughts.

EXTENDED COMMENTARY

VOLUME I, CHAPTER IX, PP. 81–3

From 'I see no reason that he should not know, as well as you' to '...trouble me with no more secrets. I'll not promise to keep them.'

These pages contain the most powerfully expressed account of the nature of love in the whole novel, while also contributing to the development of some of the novel's central thematic oppositions: joy and redemption; belonging and exclusion; constancy and transience.

For many readers, the fascination and enduring appeal of *Wuthering Heights* lies in its evocation of romantic love, the state of being utterly absorbed in another person, which can be seen as a potent, nostalgic re-enactment of the oneness experienced by mother and child before the child acquires language. This oneness is elegantly expressed by Catherine:

> My great miseries in this world have been Heathcliff's miseries, and I watched and felt each from the beginning; my great thought in living is himself. If all else perished, and *he* remained, I should still continue to be; and if all else remained, and he were annihilated, the Universe would turn to a mighty stranger. I should not seem a part of it. (p. 82)

CHECK THE BOOK **A03**

See Heather Glen's 'Critical Commentary' in her edition of *Wuthering Heights* (1988), pp. 360–1 for a good, non-technical discussion of some of these themes.

The psychologist Jacques Lacan identifies an important phase of human development as being what he calls the 'mirror phase' of infancy, in which the self is defined not through language but through the reflecting gaze of somebody else (usually the mother) who is 'more myself than I am'. Simply put, before they acquire language, children identify so powerfully with their mothers that they fail to see the difference between themselves and the mother.

Psychoanalytic readings of *Wuthering Heights* have made much of this theory. Yet because the novel is, necessarily, bound in words, it can only use words to describe this pre-verbal state. This results in the passionate statement from Catherine, which is, strictly speaking, linguistic non-sense: 'I am Heathcliff' (p. 82).

The question of whether or not this story is the most perfect example of a love story is a controversial one. Central to our understanding of the story is how we respond to the question of love. Is it love that characterises the relationship between Catherine and Heathcliff or is it, more perplexingly, just passion? If it is love, then theirs is a love which leads them to identify so much with each other, and share their feelings so deeply, that the intense identification becomes fatal. If it is love, then it is a love which requires the absolute absence of the self. If it is love, then it is a love so beyond the conventions of romantic love, in that it becomes at the end an erotic obsession with death that is ultimately repellent.

The potency of the relationship between Catherine and Heathcliff brings to the novel its focus for examining the boundaries of identity. When Catherine declares to Nelly that she is Heathcliff, she offers a radical challenge to conventional notions of selfhood and individuality. Catherine's identification with Heathcliff in this passage utterly overwhelms her own individual personal identity.

This asks a profound philosophical question: what happens to identity when individuality collides with love, in whatever form: sexual, romantic or religious? For Catherine, this can be read as a stark choice about survival. Marriage to Heathcliff would not only exclude her from a traditional Christian version of heaven but would also threaten her ability to survive in an earthly, social context. As a daughter who could not expect to inherit any property, she rightly comments that her economic and social survival depends on marriage.

Nelly Dean's role in this passage is also significant, for where Catherine's impassioned declarations of love, and marriage, are instinctive, Nelly provides the rationalist counterpart. She makes it clear that Catherine's reasons for marriage are bad ones, and crucially she points out that Catherine's wish to marry Edgar and maintain her relationship with Heathcliff is both impractical and unprincipled:

> and if *you* are his choice, he'll be the most unfortunate creature that ever was born! As soon as you become Mrs Linton, he loses friend, and love, and all! Have you considered how you'll bear the separation and how he'll bear to be quite deserted in the world? (pp. 81–2)

Catherine agrees to marry Edgar Linton, not for love, but for social mobility. Linton will offer her security in ways that she perceives to be impossible for Heathcliff: 'if Heathcliff and I married, we should be beggars' (p. 82).

Further down the page, Catherine declares:

> My love for Linton is like the foliage in the woods. Time will change it, I'm well aware, as winter changes the trees – my love for Heathcliff resembles the eternal rocks beneath – a source of little visible delight, but necessary.

Catherine perceives her real, eternal, underlying life as being inextricably bound to Heathcliff. By contrast, her feelings for Edgar Linton are subject to change and are impermanent. Catherine perceives her love for Heathcliff to be unquestionable, a given fact. Like the earth or the sky, it is part of the fundamental texture of her life. It is worth noting that the contrasting images are both drawn from the real, natural world that Catherine perceives around her, and are therefore offered up as being authentically and unarguably true.

Through the character of Catherine in this passage, passionately committed to nature, but living in the midst of the culture that defines her, Brontë challenges the opposition of culture and nature, male and female, that were being fiercely debated in the period in which Brontë was writing. Nature was traditionally linked with the female and culture with the male realm, yet Catherine is presented here as an object of exchange within the social contract of marriage and therefore central to the perpetuation of the cultural as opposed to the natural world. Her role remains a fairly passive one – her choice is between two men, only one of whom can provide a secure future, and the idea of remaining unmarried as an independent woman is not even contemplated.

Yet the desire that characterises the love between Catherine and Heathcliff is likened to 'the eternal rocks' – beyond the realms of both masculine culture and nature in its traditionally feminine, tame form. It is described as having no need of words; it is beyond language. Situated between nature and culture, participating in both and owing an allegiance to neither, the characters of Catherine and Heathcliff can be read as a challenge to that established opposition.

CRITICAL VIEWPOINT A03

It can be argued that this dilemma lies at the heart of Catherine's choice: without Heathcliff she could not exist as herself, but without a legitimate social role and position, neither she nor Heathcliff could live at all.

VOLUME I, CHAPTER X

SUMMARY

- Catherine Earnshaw is now married to Edgar Linton and lives in relative luxury and peace, indulged by Edgar and his sister Isabella.
- Heathcliff returns to the area, to Catherine's immense joy. Nelly remarks upon the transformation of Heathcliff into a tall, well-built, intelligent man.
- Heathcliff reveals that he is staying with Hindley Earnshaw at the Heights, which causes Nelly to be suspicious.
- Isabella develops an intense infatuation for Heathcliff, which he does not return. Nevertheless, he sees that he might use her feelings for him as a way to revenge himself upon Edgar.

ANALYSIS

HEATHCLIFF'S ENERGY

The return of Heathcliff to the text restores to it some of its sinister energy. It also seems to enliven Catherine and Isabella, taking them out of the atmosphere of Thrushcross Grange and onto the moors or up to the Heights. The return of Heathcliff also reinforces the truth of Catherine's insight in the previous chapter – 'If I were in heaven, Nelly, I should be extremely miserable' (p. 80) – for her soul is the same as Heathcliff's, 'and Linton's is as different as a moonbeam from lightning, or frost from fire' (p. 81). The energy of Heathcliff is a burning elemental energy which reinvigorates the **narrative** tension.

LOVE AND REVENGE

Revenge might seem to be one of the main motivating factors in this novel, yet close analysis of Heathcliff's character shows that almost always revenge is secondary to Heathcliff's overriding love of Catherine. Everything that he does has to do with reuniting him with Catherine. However, Brontë is always alive to the financial realities of her characters, and another important element of Heathcliff's revenge has to do with avarice and property.

STUDY FOCUS: ANGELS AND DEVILS A02

Towards the end of this chapter Catherine reiterates the association of Thrushcross Grange with heaven when she describes Isabella's eyes: 'They are dove's eyes – angel's' (p. 107). This, with its echo of an early description of Edgar as dove-like, prompts Heathcliff to consider the structures of inheritance, and thus form a plan for revenge. Heathcliff, a 'fierce, pitiless, wolfish man' (p. 103), who is described as a 'bird of bad omen' (p. 103) by Nelly, a 'knave' who laughs at any 'divil's jest' by Joseph (p. 104), and an 'evil beast' (p. 107) again by Nelly, is by his own admission 'ghoulish' (p. 106). All these descriptions are ranged against Isabella, who is described as a canary, a dove and an egg. However, Brontë is clear that these distinctions are not simple, as Isabella is also described as a tigress and a vixen (both p. 106), and it is Catherine who seeds the idea in Heathcliff's head about inheritance, when she announces: 'It lies in your own power to be Edgar's brother' (p. 105).

CHECK THE BOOK A04

Ian Brinton's analysis of *Wuthering Heights* (Continuum, 2010) offers a sustained reading of the relationship between revenge and greed (pp. 60–8).

GLOSSARY

92 **sizar's place** scholarship position at University

94 **sough** ditch

104 **Crahnr's 'quest** coroner's inquest (into an unnatural death)

104 **t'grand 'sizes** the Grand Assizes; here, the Day of Judgement

104 **girn** snarl

104 **pikes** gates

VOLUME I, CHAPTER XI

SUMMARY

- Nelly returns on a whim to the Heights and is appalled to see how it has deteriorated.
- Hareton, previously her charge and joy, though still barely more than five years old, curses her.
- Heathcliff calls at the Grange and makes overtures to Isabella, displeasing both Catherine and Edgar.
- Fierce arguments between Catherine, Edgar and Heathcliff induce Catherine to retire to her bed.

ANALYSIS

TWO HOUSEHOLDS

Reminiscence marks the opening of this chapter, as Nelly Dean fondly remembers both her own childhood with Hindley and her affection for Hareton. Wuthering Heights again appears as the site of brutality and revenge. This is in marked contrast to the luxury and calm of the Grange. Heathcliff, it emerges, has set son against father and is inciting revolt in the already unhappy household. At the same time, Heathcliff's next visit to the Grange sees him capitalise upon Isabella's affection. This is an important chapter when considering whether or not Heathcliff is a truly vengeful character as we see his effect on both households.

HOT AND COLD

The relationship between Catherine and Edgar is once again considered in terms of extremes of temper and temperature – 'your veins are full of ice-water – but mine are boiling' (p. 117) – and Catherine retires to her bed claiming herself to be 'in danger of being seriously ill' (p. 116). Forced to choose between Edgar and Heathcliff, she threatens to break their hearts by breaking her own (p. 116). Nelly treats Catherine's outburst as histrionics and fails to take her threatened illness seriously. Catherine departs to her room and refuses any nourishment for the next two days. Edgar retires to the library and tries to dissuade Isabella from her infatuation with Heathcliff, claiming that if she continues in it he will disown her. Who to love and the financial implications of that decision are revealed to be stark choices for women in the novel, as passion is contrasted with calm rationality and the promise of security.

STUDY FOCUS: HEATHCLIFF'S TORMENT **A03**

Heathcliff has returned dominant and physically superior to the other characters, but his life is tormented. He accuses Catherine of treating him 'infernally' and of torturing him to death for [her] amusement (p. 112). From now on there is scarcely a chapter that does not make some reference to him as suffering the torments of a lost soul. This idea of the soul being separate from the body and its development into the notion of ghosts troubling the living because there is no peace for them in death is powerfully present throughout the novel.

GRADE BOOSTER **A01**

Using appropriate critical vocabulary will enhance your grade. Make sure your references are clear and to the point.

GLOSSARY

108 **sand-pillar** milestone

109 **barn** child

VOLUME I, CHAPTER XII

SUMMARY

- Catherine is genuinely ill, having starved herself and worked herself into a fervour of ill health.
- Edgar is kept ignorant of Catherine's condition and spends his time reading. When he finally visits her room he finds her hallucinating and feverish and blames Nelly for her deterioration.
- Nelly discovers Isabella's favourite dog hanging from a tree, nearly dead.
- Nelly summons the doctor to attend Catherine, and the doctor informs her that Isabella and Heathcliff have been having secret nightly trysts and intend to elope.
- Isabella leaves Thrushcross Grange secretly to marry Heathcliff.
- On discovering her disappearance, Edgar disowns Isabella.

CONTEXT A03

The **Romantic** view is that illness gives a heightened sense of awareness, and promotes a state of higher consciousness. Catherine, Isabella and later Cathy all use this to their own advantage. Evidently this is a risky, ultimately fatal strategy for both Catherine and Isabella.

ANALYSIS

SECRETS AND MADNESS

Critical attention might first be devoted to the role of Nelly Dean in this chapter, since she is the person who controls all the key information: Catherine's illness and Isabella's departure. Secrets are the things that move the action of the book forward, and Nelly's choice to keep them or divulge them gives her immense influence over events.

Nelly's assumption that Catherine's illness is invented by her in order to manipulate others gives credence to the reading that women in the nineteenth century could use frailty as a strength. However, it is a strategy which Brontë shows to have devastating consequences.

CONTEXT A04

The reference to pigeon feathers alludes to a superstition that the soul of a dying person could not leave the body if the mattress or pillow was stuffed with pigeon feathers.

Secrecy is all about knowledge. Edgar is kept ignorant of Catherine's illness. Catherine does not know that Edgar is ignorant and cannot understand his apparent cold-heartedness. She perceives it as a want of love. Neither Catherine nor Edgar knows that Isabella has eloped. They both perceive her absence as a lack of proper affection. This agonising perception of lovelessness immediately precedes Catherine's fervent plucking out of the feathers from her pillows. **Psychoanalytic** readings have seen this type of 'madness', identified by Nelly as a 'maniac's' (p. 129) behaviour, as both a symptom and an effect of oppression.

As Joyce Carol Oates notes in an article entitled 'The Magnanimity of Wuthering Heights' (*Critical Enquiry*, 1983):

> Her passion for Heathcliff notwithstanding, Catherine's identification is with the frozen and peopleless void of an irrecoverable past, and not with anything human. The feathers she pulls out of her pillow are of course the feathers of dead, wild birds, moorcocks and lapwings: they compel her to think not of the exuberance of childhood, but of death, and even premature death, which is associated with her companion Heathcliff.

A KEY PASSAGE

Look at the passage on page 122 where Catherine plucks the feathers from her pillow and connects the fate of the birds to Heathcliff. This passage can be read as another allegory, another story about the story. The **anecdote** of the lapwings echoes Heathcliff's's own abandonment after his parents die, and also prefigures Catherine's grave upon the moors.

A **Marxist** or **new historicist** view, however, would argue that madness is itself ideologically determined. The reference to the pigeon feathers connects Catherine with the ideas of natural spirituality or superstition that are in direct conflict with the dominant discourse of Christianity. This suggests that her 'madness', like her free spirit, is a rebellion against society and its rules.

Feminist readings of the passage may read Catherine's madness here as a condition of proper femininity, the effect of domesticity and of being a wife and mother. That marriage and civilised life is not suited to Catherine is identified early on in Chapter IX, when she interprets her dream. Her pregnancy can be read as one of the causes of the arguments between Heathcliff and herself which leads her to fall ill. Her 'madness', according to such readings, is caused by the very aspects of her life that are supposed to identify her as a 'proper woman'.

STUDY FOCUS: MADNESS AND IMPRISONMENT (A03)

The feminist critics Gilbert and Gubar see the madness as a result of Catherine's imprisonment. Being trapped in her marriage to Edgar thoroughly disables Catherine. She can no longer make sense of the world, sees things entirely from her own perspective, and ultimately is confined to her bed with illness. This relationship between madness and imprisonment is common to many **Gothic** tales and **Romantic** poems, notably Byron's 'Prisoner of Chillon' and some of Emily Brontë's Gondal poems.

KEY QUOTATION: VOLUME I, CHAPTER XII (A01)

Key quotation:

'"Among his books!" she cried, confounded. "And I dying! I on the brink of the grave! My God! does he know how I'm altered?" continued she, staring at her reflection in a mirror, hanging against the opposite wall.' (p. 121)

Possible interpretations:

- Edgar's retirement to the library after the confrontation between himself and Heathcliff, and his ignorance of Catherine's illness, can be seen as part of the conflict between experience and culture in the novel. Edgar counters his interaction with the real by submerging himself in literature. Such a critical position of course assumes that literature is not part of the 'real'.
- Catherine's incredulity that Edgar continues to occupy himself with his books while she is dying once more highlights the discrepancy in values between the two houses of Nature and Culture.
- Catherine's failure to recognise her face in the mirror lends itself to a **psychoanalytic** reading as it suggests that she rejects her own identity.

REVISION FOCUS: TASK 4 (A02) (A03)

How far do you agree with the following statements?

- Emily Brontë's representations of nature are always symbolic.
- In *Wuthering Heights* madness is portrayed as a dysfunction of society, not of the mind.

Write opening paragraphs for essays based on these discussion points. Set out your arguments clearly.

CHECK THE BOOK (A03)

This passage about the birds is also closely reminiscent of Ophelia's soliloquy in *Hamlet*, where in her mad grief she counts all the flowers.

CRITICAL VIEWPOINT (A03)

Critical attention has focused upon the role of illness as a sign for femininity in the nineteenth century. Emily Brontë can be seen to be writing about illness as a female strategy here: rather than indicating simply weakness, illness becomes a way for Catherine to influence the actions of both Edgar and Heathcliff.

GLOSSARY

122 **swells** small hills
123 **elf-bolts** flint arrow-heads

VOLUME I, CHAPTER XIII

SUMMARY

- Catherine is diagnosed as having brain-fever and is nursed devotedly by Edgar, under whose care she slowly begins to improve.
- For two months Isabella and Heathcliff remain absent.
- Six weeks after their departure, Isabella writes to Edgar a letter which ends with a secret pencilled note begging for reconciliation. He ignores the request.
- She then writes to Nelly, and Nelly now reads this letter to Lockwood.
- It says that Isabella and Heathcliff are back at Wuthering Heights as Hindley is intent on winning back from Heathcliff all the money he has lost to him through gambling.
- In the letter, Isabella perceives herself to be both friendless and abused in her relationship with Heathcliff.
- Isabella describes how Hindley showed her a gun with which he intended to kill Heathcliff, and her reaction to this weapon is one of covetousness rather than horror.
- The letter details Heathcliff's reaction on hearing of Catherine's illness for which he blames Edgar, promising that Isabella shall be her proxy in suffering.
- The letter and the chapter end with an entreaty from Isabella to Nelly Dean to call on her at Wuthering Heights.

ANALYSIS

ILLNESS AND STRENGTH

At the beginning of this chapter Catherine is sick with a fever brought on by mental anguish. She is diagnosed as having brain-fever. Susan Sontag has written persuasively about the use of illness as a cultural **metaphor** in *Illness as Metaphor and Aids and its Metaphors* (1989): 'Brain-fever might well be thought of as the disease of someone who is a "creature of passionate extremes, someone too sensitive to bear the horrors of the vulgar everyday world"' (p. 36). Critical analysis of this chapter has focused on Catherine's entrapment in a way of life which is counter to her natural values, an imprisonment that literally makes her sick.

Isabella's inability to partake of the food at Wuthering Heights because it is too coarse for her can be read as indicative of her unlikeliness to be nourished or sustained by life with Heathcliff. Like Catherine's refusal of food at the Grange it can be seen as a hostile strategy of control, which is used as a method of punishment.

STUDY FOCUS: VIOLENCE AND THE GUN (A03)

The reference to the gun, which Isabella views with desire rather than horror, is again indicative that violence is as much a part of the civilised life (which Isabella has hitherto represented) as it is a part of the rude brutality of the Heights. Isabella's devotion to Heathcliff results in her destruction and despair, and this is contrasted both with Edgar's devotion to Catherine, and with Catherine's choice of social status over passion.

Feminist theorists have devoted some attention to the gun which Isabella desires, and the whip requested by Catherine at the beginning if the novel, reading both of these as phallic symbols. It is important to note that as phallic symbols they signify desire not for the penis as such, but for the power the penis represents. As many feminist critics have pointed out, all the economic power in the institution of marriage as it is described in this novel resides with the men.

CHECK THE BOOK (A04)

For a collection of feminist critical essays on power in literature and society, see Mills et al., *Feminist Readings, Feminist Reading* (1989).

GLOSSARY

137	**mim**	prim
137	**minching and munching**	affected ways
141	**flitting**	moving house
141	**thible**	stirring stick or spoon
141	**nave**	fist
141	**pale t' guilp off**	skim the froth off
141	**deaved aht**	knocked out
142	**meeterly**	properly
142	**mells**	meddles
143	**madling**	fool
143	**pining**	starving
143	**plisky**	tantrum

VOLUME I, CHAPTER XIV

SUMMARY

- Nelly goes to see Isabella as requested and informs Edgar of Isabella's predicament, but Edgar refuses to have anything to do with her.
- Heathcliff determines to see Catherine whether permission is granted or not, and Nelly reluctantly agrees to act as intermediary.
- Time switches to the present. The doctor calls on Lockwood, and Lockwood reflects that he must be cautious of falling in love with the present Catherine for fear that she should resemble the first.

ANALYSIS

EDGAR

Edgar's coldness, referred to often by Catherine, now emerges as a cold-hearted indifference to his sister's plight; he refuses the more fiery emotion of anger. He says he is sorry to have lost her, but insists that communication between him and Isabella will no longer exist. Whereas Heathcliff and Catherine maintain their passionate connection, and feel that were one to die the other would inhabit a living hell, Edgar suffers no such attachment to Isabella and symbolically kills her: 'we are eternally divided' (p. 145).

ISABELLA

Isabella's position as a dependant of Heathcliff is made clear in two passages: first, when Heathcliff asserts the lengths he has gone to in order to prevent Isabella claiming a separation (p. 149). In fact the effort would not have been considerable since, as John Stuart Mill notes in *The Subjection of Women* (1869), the position of women within marriage was worse than that of slaves. The second passage makes reference to Isabella's mental health (p. 150) and the practice of incarcerating women as mentally ill, notwithstanding any evidence to the contrary. Here we see Brontë's sensitivity to the ways in which power is neither generous nor neutral. It is up for grabs, and Heathcliff makes ample use of this fact, incarcerating Isabella at Wuthering Heights, keeping her isolated and apart in a duplicate world with special rules over which he has sole control.

Isabella, in spite of her much reduced and saddened circumstances at the Heights, nevertheless displays a violent streak that subverts the expected behaviour of a woman of her status: 'The single pleasure I can imagine is to die, or to see him dead' (p. 151).

STUDY FOCUS: DIFFERENT PERSPECTIVES · A02

Lockwood typically draws the wrong conclusion from Nelly Dean's story when he assumes that she is warning him against becoming too enthralled with Cathy Heathcliff, for Nelly Dean sees marriage to someone else as the only escape for Cathy and is eager to find her another husband. Lockwood, once again, represents exactly the supersensitive, precious world of the educated, or cultured, which is here contrasted with the world of passion and experience. Lockwood's illness situates him as profoundly disconnected from mundane reality, or daily life. Here Brontë cautions us against identifying too closely with the views of either narrator.

GRADE BOOSTER · A02

Referring to the structural use of the two **narrators** to make and contrast different meanings will impress your examiner.

CHECK THE BOOK · A04

John Stuart Mill's *The Subjection of Women* (1869) provides an interesting, almost contemporary account of the place and role of women in Victorian society. Emily Brontë sets her novel earlier, at the very end of eighteenth century, but the plight of her female characters was exactly the situation which prompted Mill to write on this issue.

GLOSSARY

150 **brach** she-dog; bitch

153 **dree** cheerless

VOLUME II, CHAPTER I

SUMMARY

- Lockwood takes up the **narrative** again, but speaks as though he were Nelly Dean.
- Nelly returns to Thrushcross Grange and arranges matters so that the household is empty apart from herself and Catherine, in order that Heathcliff may pay his visit.
- The narrative recommences with Heathcliff's visit to Catherine.
- On seeing Catherine, Heathcliff despairs, perceiving that she is pregnant and that she is certainly going to die. The conversation and interaction between Catherine and Heathcliff ricochets between love and death, and they fall on each other in a passionate embrace, while talking of going to the grave.
- Catherine faints in Heathcliff's arms just as Edgar Linton enters. When they finally manage to revive Catherine, Heathcliff has departed but resolves to stay in the garden until Nelly can bring him news of Catherine.

ANALYSIS

NELLY'S ROLE

Nelly is once again a catalyst for action as she traffics between Wuthering Heights and Thrushcross Grange. The narration, which throughout has properly belonged to Lockwood, as the opening to this second volume reminds us, is nevertheless more credibly Nelly Dean's.

SEX AND DEATH

The opening chapter of this second volume highlights the drama of the conflicts and correspondences between sexuality and death. It is possible to draw parallels between the concerns of this chapter and concerns which dominate Emily Brontë's poetry, not least the longing to escape this world, through either love or death.

Reading retrospectively, it is possible to see Heathcliff's despair upon seeing Catherine as again being provoked not only by his perception of her certain death, but also by his perception of her pregnancy, since his words are 'Oh, Cathy! Oh, my life! how can I bear it?' (p. 160), and we only have Nelly's interpretation of his anguish as being that Catherine was 'fated, sure to die'. Such a reading supports the **structuralist** argument that sees an association between sex and death. This is quite a complex argument but, in its most simplistic form, if sex is seen as similar to death in that it involves the absolute surrender of the body, then there is clearly a way in which Catherine's pregnancy is as abhorrent to Heathcliff as her impending death.

STUDY FOCUS: LOVE AND CLASS

A **Marxist** or **new historicist** reading of this chapter might look at the manner in which Heathcliff is economically transformed and the impact that this has upon his emotional relationship with Catherine. It could be argued that Catherine rejects his new persona, and her assertion 'That is not *my* Heathcliff. I shall love mine yet' (p. 161) sites Heathcliff as an opponent of, and not the embodiment of, bourgeois values.

VOLUME II, CHAPTER II

SUMMARY

- Catherine's daughter Cathy is born the same night, two months prematurely.
- Catherine dies in childbirth and Edgar is so stricken with grief that he cannot welcome his daughter.
- Heathcliff knows the news even before Nelly tells him, and cries out that he cannot live without Catherine.
- The funeral takes place a week later. Hindley Earnshaw (Catherine's brother) is invited but Isabella (her sister-in-law) is not.
- Catherine is buried on a grassy slope in a corner of the graveyard nearest the moor.

ANALYSIS

THE IMPACT OF CATHERINE'S DEATH

Heathcliff's response to Catherine's death – that she is his life and soul (p.169) — echoes her previous declaration of love for him in Volume I, Chapter IX. Similarly, his declaration comes just as she has departed and no action can be taken. But Brontë is at pains to demonstrate that their love transcends conventional boundaries, and the **Gothic** delight in ghosts and the supernatural here finds its supreme articulation in Heathcliff's declaration: 'I know that ghosts *have* wandered on earth. Be with me always – take any form – drive me mad' (p. 169). Edgar's response is to sleep, alongside his dead wife, in 'exhausted anguish' (p. 166), a sleep which seems to prefigure Heathcliff's desire to open her coffin and sleep with her in Chapter XV. Both these loves, Brontë suggests, are profound enough to extend beyond death.

KEY QUOTATION: VOLUME II, CHAPTER II A01

Key quotation:

'The place of Catherine's interment … was neither in the chapel, under the carved monument of the Lintons, nor yet by the tombs of her own relations, outside. It was dug on a green slope, in a corner of the kirkyard, where the wall is so low that heath and bilberry plants have climbed over it from the moor; and peat mould almost buries it. Her husband lies in the same spot, now.' (p. 170)

Possible interpretations:

- Catherine's burial place, almost on the moor itself, lies exactly between the two different versions of holy ground that Brontë posits in the novel: the moor and the churchyard.
- Catherine is buried beyond the plots of her families (birth and marriage). She is outside their frame. This enables her to enter her kingdom of Heaven (the moor) and reconnect beyond the grave with Heathcliff.
- Edgar chooses to be buried with his wife rather than in his family tomb, thus signifying his great love for her.

EXTENDED COMMENTARY

VOLUME II, CHAPTER II, PP. 166–9

From 'About twelve o'clock, that night...' to 'He was beyond my skill to quiet or console.'

This is an important chapter, which acts as a hinge between the two volumes. The death of Catherine and the birth of Cathy enable all the structural repetitions which are such an important feature of *Wuthering Heights*.

The death of Catherine highlights some important issues. Primarily, it points to the powerful nature of Heathcliff's love for Catherine, which he believes extends beyond the grave. A historical reading of the chapter would also highlight the dangers of childbirth for women in the nineteenth century.

Nelly Dean also comments upon the consequences of Catherine's death for the inheritance laws. Old Mr Linton has bequeathed his property to Isabella, and subsequently to her male offspring should Edgar fail to have a son.

C. P. Sanger has commented upon the very detailed knowledge that Brontë displays of the inheritance laws of the nineteenth century. This knowledge is crucial to the plot of *Wuthering Heights* since, according to this law, Catherine Linton cannot inherit Thrushcross Grange when her father dies. Instead, the property automatically passes to the male progeny of Isabella. However, should there be no male progeny, or should that son die, the property would then revert to Catherine Linton. It is for this reason that Heathcliff is so intent upon the marriage between Catherine and Linton, for as his daughter-in-law her property becomes his.

The passage starts with the birth of Cathy, born two months prematurely, and two hours before the death of her mother. Nelly describes Cathy as a 'feeble orphan'. Scarcely any child is born in this novel without it becoming an orphan, and indeed all the mothers die apart from Nelly, who acts as a surrogate mother to everyone except Linton. This can be linked with Emily Brontë's own lived experience, since her mother died  when she was three years old. Cathy is born into a family in grief, unwelcomed, a child for whom 'nobody cared a morsel … We redeemed the neglect afterwards; but its beginning was as friendless as its end is likely to be' (p. 166).

Childbirth, as an experience belonging to the private sphere of womanhood, has traditionally been marginalised in literature. Here, however, Brontë focuses on childbirth as a life-changing event, indeed a life-threatening event for Catherine, resulting in her death. A feminist reading of this passage might focus on the impact upon identity for a woman carrying and then giving birth to a child. The bodily experience of giving birth raises questions of self and other, identity and individuality – two individuals are bound together in one body, which then divides to produce two distinct identities. Brontë highlights this unity and subsequent duality by naming both individuals Catherine. The tragic death of Catherine shortly after giving birth leaves a child without a mother, a single Catherine without her counterpart.

The second part of the excerpt details Nelly's recollection of finding Edgar Linton the next morning lying asleep next to his dead wife. This is a significant passage, for it reminds us of the strength of Edgar's feelings for Catherine, so often overshadowed by Heathcliff's. In death, they are united in an infinite calm, which is in direct contrast to Heathcliff's anguish and torment. Nelly's account sees them lying in 'Divine rest', as though Catherine were already an angel in heaven. While in Edgar's domain, Catherine's life (and death) is perceived as peaceful and full of propriety. This supports Edgar's decision, much later, to be buried next to Catherine on the edge of the moor.

Nelly's account of her own Christian piety in the face of death establishes Brontë's complex relationship with the conventional Victorian view of death and heaven. Nelly's account, though sentimental, is honourable. Brontë does not ridicule the conventional view, even though she pits it against a much more robust and challenging idea of what Paradise might be.

When Nelly asks Lockwood what he calls a 'heterodox' question about whether people such as Catherine could be happy in the other world, she identifies herself as someone who is potentially sympathetic to the possibility of the more unconventional vision being true, and it is this which makes her the ideal go-between for Catherine and Heathcliff in the previous chapters.

The next passage is one of the most dramatic exchanges between Heathcliff and Nelly, and covers Heathcliff's reaction to the news that Catherine is dead. The most striking thing to begin with is that Heathcliff already knows. He has been standing against an old ash tree, and he is so at one with it that the blackbirds (ousels) pay him no attention.

Symbolically, trees signify endurance, and balance between spiritual and earthly. The tree shows us how, from a tiny seed of potential, a great soul can come into being. This is entirely in keeping with Brontë's view of heaven being as one with nature. Heathcliff is at peace with the knowledge of Catherine's death when Nelly approaches him: 'She's dead! ... I've not waited for you to learn that. Put your handkerchief away – don't snivel before me. Damn you all! she wants none of *your* tears!' (p. 168).

It is only when confronted with the conventional Christian version of her death and her peace that Heathcliff flies into a passion, which causes him to bleed in agony.

Brontë's account can be read as almost a crucifixion of Heathcliff. He is against the tree; he is in silent combat with his inner agony; it is as if he is 'goaded to death with knives and spears' (p. 169). His hand and forehead are stained with blood. He calls upon Catherine not to abandon him in the abyss.

Brontë also makes much of Heathcliff's animal passion in this passage, in direct contrast to the reaction of Edgar to Catherine's death, which is no less keenly felt. Heathcliff is referred to as a 'creature', 'ferocious', howling 'not like a man, but like a savage beast' (p. 169).

The other thing to note in this passage is Nelly's description of the moment of death: 'Her life closed in a gentle dream' (p. 169). This is extraordinary, for nowhere else in the novel are dreams referred to as gentle. Dreams are almost always disturbing and unsettling, prescient of danger or illness, and Nelly is afraid of them.

GRADE BOOSTER **A02**

Watch out for key points of language that you can analyse for AO2. Here, the bestial terminology that Brontë uses to describe Heathcliff's raw pain seems appropriate to the cruelty and lack of human feeling he will display in the rest of the volume.

VOLUME II, CHAPTER III

SUMMARY

- Nelly acts as surrogate mother to the baby Cathy.
- Hindley dies shortly after Catherine, leaving the Heights mortgaged in gambling debts to Heathcliff.
- Isabella leaves Heathcliff and goes to the South of England where, a few months later, her son Linton is born.
- Isabella dies when Linton is twelve.
- Heathcliff, now living alone at the Heights with the disinherited Hareton, learns of his son's birth through the servants' gossip.

ANALYSIS

A BROKEN MARRIAGE

The chapter begins when Isabella bursts in on Nelly at Thrushcross Grange unannounced, having run away from Heathcliff. As the Marxist-feminist critic Lynne Pearce points out in her essay 'Sexual Politics', when Isabella eventually flees the Heights it is indeed as a 'battered wife' (in Mills et al., 1989, p. 36). Pearce draws our attention to the very explicit nature of violence against women in this novel, arguing that it is a 'manifestation of patriarchy by force at its most extreme' (p. 36).

Isabella is en route to the South, having fled Heathcliff and the Heights. She throws her wedding ring into the fire and describes the living conditions at the Heights as both physically and morally corrupt. If we are to accept Pearce's reading, then, this jettisoning of her wedding ring is not merely Isabella's rejection of her marriage to Heathcliff, but a profound rejection of the entire oppressive institution of marriage as experienced by a relatively wealthy middle-class woman in the nineteenth  century. Isabella gives a full and florid account of the violence she both witnesses and suffers at the Heights, so much so that she makes but a casual reference to Hareton hanging a litter of puppies from the chair back, whereas previously her relationship with her own dog (which Heathcliff hanged) was profound and tender-hearted.

HEATHCLIFF'S TRANSFORMATION

Heathcliff has now gained control of Wuthering Heights, having originally arrived as a presumed orphan, and having been humiliated by his lack of proper status. Critics have read this transformation in a number of ways.

A **Marxist** reading of it could see it as the triumph of capitalism over a belated feudalism in which competition becomes the new tyranny, since it is only through the acquisition of wealth that Heathcliff manages to move from the margins of society to its centre, infiltrating its institutions of marriage and property ownership and appropriating them for his own ends.

A **Romanticist** reading might emphasise the fact that Heathcliff has transformed his fortunes through his passionate dedication to feeding his 'greedy jealousy' for Catherine. Hareton, who should be the Heights' rightful inheritor, is dependent upon Heathcliff, who uses the opportunity to repeat the abuse that he himself suffered as someone of no social property.

STUDY FOCUS: NELLY'S GRIEF (A02)

It is worth remarking Nelly's disproportionate grief upon hearing of Hindley's death: 'I confess this blow was greater to me than the shock of Mrs Linton's death: ancient associations lingered round my heart; I sat down in the porch, and wept as for a blood relation' (p. 186). Nelly's grief at the news of Hindley's death emphasises the tight structural pairings in this novel. Nelly and Hindley, Heathcliff and Catherine, and Isabella and Edgar all grow up in more or less fraternal relationships. Nelly's mother was in fact Hindley's wet nurse, so they did literally share 'mother's milk'. With Nelly's grief we see Brontë once again making a critical comparison between genuine heartfelt feelings of loss and grief and the formal requirements of institutionalised religion, and this scene is reminiscent of the grief demonstrated by Catherine and Heathcliff when their 'father' dies.

THE DEATH OF HINDLEY

The death of Hindley has also been the site of much critical commentary, some of it to do with chronological correctness. Barbara Gates has argued that Brontë's novel draws freely on laws and customs which post-date the setting of her story (1771–1803). In narrating the details surrounding Hindley Earnshaw's death (1784), for example, she draws upon statutes which relate to early Victorian customs. Although the precise cause of Hindley's death is never determined, all reports claim that he died in a state of drunkenness. Kenneth, who informs Nelly of the death, is clear and claims that he 'died true to his character, drunk as a lord' (p. 186).

Heathcliff, when Nelly asks if she may proceed with suitable arrangements for Hindley's funeral, retorts: 'Correctly . . . that fool's body should be buried at the cross-roads, without ceremony of any kind – I happened to leave him ten minutes, yesterday afternoon; and, in that interval, he fastened the two doors of the house against me, and he has spent the night in drinking himself to death deliberately!' (p. 187).

As Gates makes clear in her essay, the exact circumstances of Hindley's death, which Brontë records in considerable detail, have important implications for the course of the novel. If Hindley did die drunk and debauched, as both Kenneth and Heathcliff indicate that he did, then, according to eighteenth-century law and custom, he would automatically have been considered a suicide, exactly as Heathcliff suggests. Even more significantly, if that were to be the case his property could legally have been forfeited to the Crown, with nothing left for Hareton and hence nothing left for Heathcliff to employ as a tool in his revenge. It is therefore most likely for this reason that Heathcliff allows Nelly to perform proper burial rights for Hindley, thus relinquishing the immediate gratification of revenge upon Hindley's dead body for the larger rewards of power over the entire Earnshaw family.

CONTEXT (A04)

Burial at a cross-roads was traditional for suicides, who could not be buried in consecrated ground.

CONTEXT (A04)

Barbara T. Gates has a very detailed account published on the web at victorianweb.org of her analysis of suicides and burial customs in nineteenth-century England, in which she demonstrates that intimate knowledge of the laws and customs attending to death and burial has profound implications for Emily Brontë's plot.

GLOSSARY

178 **girned** snarled

187 **at the cross-roads** the place of burial for those who commit suicide

187 **taen tent** taken care

VOLUME II, CHAPTER IV

SUMMARY

- Twelve years pass, which Nelly describes as being very happy ones during which she brings up Cathy, who lives a loving and protected life at the Grange.
- Edgar receives a letter from Isabella informing him that she is dying and pleading with him to care for her son. He brings Linton home to the Grange at Isabella's request.
- During the time Edgar is away, Cathy ventures to Wuthering Heights and meets Hareton.
- Cathy is horrified to learn that Hareton is her cousin. Nelly Dean is very annoyed with Cathy and impresses upon her that she must not inform her father of her new-found knowledge or he might order Nelly to leave his employment.

ANALYSIS

HOME AS PRISON

Both the Grange and the Heights can be read as confining spaces, imprisoning this new generation of Lintons and Earnshaws. Hareton is confined by Heathcliff, who has cheated him of his inheritance and has refused him any education; and Cathy is confined by the protective nature of life at the Grange, beyond whose boundaries she is not permitted to wander. Read in terms of the conflict

between opposing forces, these confines can be seen as the limits of different kinds of knowledge. Hareton is forbidden knowledge of a formal, literary sort, and Cathy is prohibited from experiencing any life other than that which her father controls. When the two come into confrontation they can neither comprehend nor admit each other.

STUDY FOCUS: KINSHIP AND LANGUAGE   A02

That Cathy and Hareton fail to understand each other is a source of hurt and distress for both of them (p. 198), but nevertheless they do make a connection with each other, and he expands her controlled knowledge of the world by introducing her to fairy caves and 'twenty other queer places'. Once again two opposing worlds collide, but this time Brontë holds out the promise that there can be some common ground between them in this shared love of magic and nature.

VOLUME II, CHAPTER V

SUMMARY

- Isabella dies, and Edgar returns from the South of England with his nephew Linton Heathcliff.
- They no sooner arrive back at the Grange than Heathcliff demands Linton's presence at the Heights.
- Linton is described as a sickly and effeminate child, being delicate owing to ill health.
- Edgar is forced to promise to deliver the boy the following day.

ANALYSIS

PITY AND REVENGE

This chapter highlights the twin themes of pity and revenge. Edgar Linton does not wish to relinquish Linton to Heathcliff, but cannot find a way around it. However, his refusal to deliver the child immediately establishes something of Edgar's character. He is rational (in that he seeks a plan although he cannot find one) and he is forceful (in that he does not relinquish Linton immediately). Heathcliff's revenge requires Linton's presence at the Heights, so structurally we can see that the two themes are linked to the two houses: pity with Thrushcross Grange and Edgar; revenge with Wuthering Heights and Heathcliff.

STUDY FOCUS: NELLY'S LANGUAGE | A02

Nelly's language becomes more educated as she represents Edgar Linton. It is also an example of how Brontë uses the commentary of the **narrator** to articulate character. We understand something about Edgar from the form of Nelly's narration as much as from her comments.

> **GRADE BOOSTER** | A02
>
> Consider the subtleties of Brontë's use of different language styles for each of her characters in order to promote different aspects of their personalities.

KEY QUOTATION: VOLUME II, CHAPTER V | A01

Key quotation:

'While they exchanged caresses, I took a peep in to see after Linton. He was asleep, in a corner, wrapped in a warm, fur-lined cloak, as if it had been winter. A pale, delicate, effeminate boy, who might have been taken for my master's younger brother, so strong was the resemblance, but there was a sickly peevishness in his aspect, that Edgar Linton never had.' (p. 200)

Possible interpretations:

- Our first impression of Linton Heathcliff as both feeble and an invalid frustrates conventional Victorian notions of heredity since he is Heathcliff's son.
- Linton's description links to the themes of femininity/masculinity, power and ill health.
- There are also links to the wider theme of kinship and inheritance.
- The emphasis upon physical description suggests that he is not emotionally robust.
- It has been suggested that Linton has to be sickly since he is the product of a union that should never have been and is, literally, invalid.

> **GLOSSARY**
>
> 202 **baht** without
>
> 203 **nowt** nothing
>
> 203 **maks noa 'cahnt** pays no attention to
>
> 203 **norther** neither
>
> 203 **darr** dare

VOLUME II, CHAPTER VI

SUMMARY

- Nelly takes Linton to Wuthering Heights, but this is kept secret from Cathy.
- Heathcliff professes his profound disappointment in his son, but describes his ambition for Linton as being to take over all the property of both the Lintons and the Earnshaws.
- In spite of Heathcliff's vindictive avarice, Nelly takes comfort from the thought that in order to achieve this aim Heathcliff must take care of his son and provide him with the education that befits a gentleman of property.
- The contrast between Linton and Hareton is starkly drawn.
- Linton repeats Isabella's inability to eat the food at Wuthering Heights (Vol. I, Ch. XIII) as it is insufficiently delicate for him.

ANALYSIS

CONTEXT **A04**

Food also has mythic resonance. Accepting food from someone places you in their power. It is not difficult to read the refusal of food in this novel as a refusal to submit to power.

FOOD

As Philip K. Wion has noted in his psychoanalytic reading of the novel, *Wuthering Heights* is full of oral imagery. Almost all the social encounters involve food, and food is one of the signs which signals belonging and acceptance. If we persist in the reading of the two houses as representing different kinds of knowledge, then the acceptance of food represents an acceptance of a particular way of understanding life.

Food has also been seen as a sexual metaphor, incorporating as it does profound oral gratification. A delicate appetite might therefore be read as a reluctance to experience or engage with the sensual or the physical.

Food imagery in *Wuthering Heights*, then, operates simultaneously as the symbol of care and love, with Nelly frequently offering her charges plates of nourishing comfort food, and the instrument of control and authority. As such, it demonstrates neatly the difficulties critics have had in deciding whether this is a love story or a story of social manners.

GLOSSARY

209 **mucky** dirty

VOLUME II, CHAPTER VII

SUMMARY

- Cathy's disappointment at the untimely disappearance of her cousin gives way to a resigned acceptance.
- On her sixteenth birthday she encounters Heathcliff and goes with him back to Wuthering Heights, where she sees Linton again and also meets Hareton, whom she can hardly believe is also her cousin.
- She confronts her father with her new-found knowledge.
- She learns of Heathcliff's plan for revenge and agrees not to visit the Heights again, but nevertheless conspires to find a way to correspond with Linton.

ANALYSIS

LETTERS AND LEARNING

Critical attention has frequently focused on the role of letters and education in this novel, and this chapter highlights these issues. This is a novel which abounds with forbidden texts, from Catherine's diaries through to Cathy's love letters. Text comes to represent knowledge, and Hareton is abused for his lack of it or for his inability to control it. Hareton's inability to read the sign above his own front door is symbolic of his inability to read the situation in which Heathcliff is cheating him of his rightful inheritance.

STUDY FOCUS: EDUCATION `A04`

This chapter highlights Brontë's view of the role of education, which is seen as both a liberator and a form of social control. This links to the themes of different, exclusive kinds of knowledge and power. All the characters in the novel, including its two narrators, are readers in one sense or another, needing to make sense of the signs before them. Hareton's lack of education is precisely what disempowers him. The route to reconciliation and resolution is through Hareton acquiring an education via Cathy.

KEY QUOTATION: VOLUME II, CHAPTER VII `A01`

Key quotation:

'I was still surprised to discover that they were a mass of correspondence, daily almost, it must have been, from Linton Heathcliff, answers to documents forwarded by her. The earlier dated were embarrassed and short; gradually, however, they expanded into copious love letters, foolish as the age of the writer rendered natural, yet with touches, here and there, which I thought were borrowed from a more experienced source.' (p. 225)

Possible interpretations:

- This highlights the role of the written word in the novel and links to the forbidden texts of letters and diaries that abound throughout.
- It emphasises Nelly's role as go-between and facilitator of social relationships.
- It also comfirms Nelly as an astute reader of signs, able to distinguish nuances of sophistication.

CHECK THE BOOK `A04`

Linda Peterson (1992) observes in her introduction to a critical edition of *Wuthering Heights* that Brontë seems ambivalent about the effects of education. On the one hand, the denial of education is seen as a form of social punishment; on the other, the conventional forms of nineteenth-century education are frequently pitted against power, both sexual and physical.

GLOSSARY

214 **nab** a jutting hill or rock. Often this term comes to name a particular piece of hill or moorland.
219 **gaumless** witless, lacking in understanding
219 **faster** more firmly
220 **lath** weakling

VOLUME II, CHAPTER VIII

SUMMARY

- The chapter opens with another distinct reference to time, and the seasonal change. Edgar Linton develops a chill and is confined indoors.
- Cathy climbs over a wall and cannot get back.
- While she is behind the wall she again encounters Heathcliff, who informs her that Linton is dying of a broken heart owing to her abrupt termination of their correspondence.
- Cathy's sensitive nature is deeply troubled by both this news and her fears that her father will die of his chill.
- The next day Cathy sets out again, with Nelly, to see Linton.

ANALYSIS

CHECK THE BOOK A03

Nancy Armstrong's essay 'Imperialist Nostalgia and Wuthering Heights' (1982; reprinted in Linda Peterson (ed.), *Wuthering Heights: Case Studies in Contemporary Criticism*, 1992) has some interesting things to say about framing and enclosure in the novel.

STUDY FOCUS: STRUCTURAL BOUNDARIES   A02

This chapter includes a number of structural elements that have claimed the attention of **formalist** critics. These include boundaries, illness, death and responsibility. The door to her home is locked, and Cathy becomes trapped behind a wall. Unable to get back over the wall, she is literally beyond the pale and therefore vulnerable to the dark forces of Wuthering Heights and Heathcliff.

LOVE AND DEATH

While out on the moors Cathy is morose and unable to take pleasure in the rejuvenating natural world because she is anxious about her father, and morbidly concerned with death, abandonment and whether love is enough to sustain a life. These are the primary concerns and themes of the novel as a whole, reiterated by Cathy in terms of filial love.

Heathcliff's information that Linton is dying of a broken heart is disingenuous. Linton is physically failing and Heathcliff is desirous of rekindling the love affair between Linton and Cathy – in this way he can be seen to manipulate Cathy's fear of love and death to ensure that his plans for revenge are not thwarted.

GLOSSARY

230 **starved** frozen
230 **sackless** dispirited
231 **canty** lively

VOLUME II, CHAPTER IX

SUMMARY

- Cathy and Nelly again visit Wuthering Heights to find Linton more delicate and peevish than ever.
- Cathy and Linton quarrel about the nature of marriage, and there is a long discussion about love and whether the love between Catherine and Heathcliff was greater than that between Catherine and Edgar.
- Linton persuades Cathy to return the following day. Nelly falls ill with a chill so Cathy returns to the Heights without any restrictive supervision.

ANALYSIS

DECEIT AND SECRETS

When Nelly falls ill towards the end of this chapter she comments on how well Cathy looks after her: 'like an angel' (p. 243). This links to the broader themes of good and evil, trust and deceit, and secrets in general, for in this Nelly shows an unusual incompetence at reading the signs. Cathy, however, is a true hybrid, embodying the virtues of both households, genuinely caring for the sick, but also capable of exercising her own will and judgement and going out onto the moors unsupervised.

STUDY FOCUS: ILLNESS AS STRATEGY **A02**

This is another chapter in which illness operates to forward the action of the novel. Linton Heathcliff capitalises on his own frailty to influence Cathy's movements. Later in the chapter Nelly's chill enables Cathy to go the Heights unhindered. Illness is seen as both a form of power, a means of controlling other people, and a means to gain freedom, since Cathy makes use of the fact that Nelly is too ill to accompany her to further her own strategem.

KEY QUOTATION: VOLUME II, CHAPTER IX **A01**

Key quotation:

'Linton denied that people ever hated their wives; but Cathy affirmed they did, and in her wisdom, instanced his own father's aversion to her aunt.' (p. 238)

Possible interpretations:

- It links to the broader themes of love and kinship, and who truly belongs with whom.
- It refers to Heathcliff's plan for revenge. At this point the reader (and Nelly) knows more than Cathy and Linton do.

CHECK THE BOOK A04

In her book *Victorian Writing and Working Women* (1985) Julia Swindells offers an interesting account of the relationships between medicine, health and power in the nineteenth century.

GLOSSARY

236 **elysium** a place of ideal happiness

237 **gadding off** wandering off to enjoy oneself

243 **laid up** confined to bed

VOLUME II, CHAPTER X

SUMMARY

- Once again the chapter opens with a distinct reference to time.
- Three weeks later Nelly is restored to health, much to Cathy's frustration.
- Nelly discovers Cathy's deception and Cathy confides in her the details of all her visits, most of which have been dutiful rather than pleasurable.
- There is discussion of ideal heaven between Linton and Cathy, in which she accuses his vision of being only 'half alive' and he accuses hers of being 'drunk' (p. 248).
- Hareton's attempts to read are once again the subject of mockery.
- Nelly betrays Cathy's confidence and informs Edgar of Cathy's visits, which are promptly curtailed.
- Edgar writes to Linton and invites him to the Grange.

ANALYSIS

KNOWLEDGE AND BELONGING

This chapter expands upon one of the central themes of the novel: the nature and uses of knowledge. Hareton is abused for his limited skills; Nelly Dean uses her knowledge to influence events in the novel – her betrayal of Cathy's confidences has profound consequences for the health of both Edgar and Linton, though she is unaware of this. Critics interested in the gender issues of this novel have commented upon this emphasis on Edgar's and Linton's illnesses as serving to feminise them.

The argument about heaven is indicative of a reversal in the natures of the Grange and the Heights, since Linton's view is constricted and peaceful, and Cathy's sparkles and dances 'in a glorious jubilee' (p. 245), suggesting that neither Linton nor Cathy are where they properly belong. This also suggests that knowledge is unstable, subject to change and revision, an argument which has profound moral consequences and is one of the reasons why Brontë's novel was considered so radical and unpalatable by Victorian readers.

> **CONTEXT** **A04**
>
> Matthew Arnold's collection of essays *Culture and Anarchy* (1869) presents a prevailing Victorian notion that culture is a moral phenomenon, the ideal of human perfection, 'sweetness and light'. Although this collection post-dates Brontë , *Wuthering Heights* can clearly be considered as engaging with this idea.

GLOSSARY		
246	**frame**	invent
248	**throstles**	thrushes
250	**conned**	learned
251	**sarve ye aht**	take revenge; serve you right
251	**skift**	move
252	**bahn**	going; here, bound

VOLUME II, CHAPTER XI

SUMMARY

- The narrative moves to the near present, events having only happened in the last year.
- Lockwood denies any romantic interest in Cathy.
- Edgar, realising that his death is imminent, commences a correspondence with Linton in an attempt to reassure himself as to Cathy's future.
- Linton too is dying but Heathcliff conceals this knowledge from Edgar.
- No one at Thrushcross Grange perceives Linton's health to be as precarious as it actually is.

ANALYSIS

LETTERS

Once again letters play a critical and unreliable part in the sequence of events. Edgar is deceived by the letters Linton sends him into thinking that his nephew is healthier than he really is – Linton is completely under Heathcliff's command by this time. It is significant that Edgar blindly trusts the principle of correspondence to reassure himself: he is of Thrushcross Grange, the 'House of Culture'. Heathcliff, on the other hand, who has received a much shadier and darker education, is more than capable of manipulating events through a series of letters. Letters in fact suit his purposes far better than face-to-face contact, which would have been more likely to reveal the extent of Linton's deterioration.

STUDY FOCUS: LOVE AND LOCKWOOD   A04

Lockwood's denial of his interest in Cathy at this point structurally repeats his account of his refusal of a 'most fascinating creature, a real goddess' (p. 6) at the beginning of the novel. His interest in women is relentlessly voyeuristic, and unrealistic. With the exception of his relationship with Nelly Dean, his interaction with women is both awkward and stilted. He is frequently to be caught peeping at them through doorways or windows. Lockwood's preference for the imagined over the real relationship can be seen as participating in one of the central struggles of the novel.

KEY QUOTATION: VOLUME II, CHAPTER XI   A01

Key quotation:

'"Ellen, I've been very happy with my little Cathy. Through winter nights and summer days she was a living hope by my side – "' (p. 257)

Possible interpretations:

- Edgar's confession that he has been happy is reminiscent of Catherine's remonstrances to Heathcliff when she is dying: 'will you be happy when I am in the earth?' (p. 160).
- Read in the light of this, it is not so much an acknowledgement of his love of his daughter as a confession of his insufficient love of Catherine.

GRADE BOOSTER   A02

To get the best grades at AS and A2 level you need to be able to demonstrate that you understand key aspects of language and form. Consider the use of letters in this novel both as a means of moving the action along and as a symbolic code for establishing power.

VOLUME II, CHAPTER XII

SUMMARY

- Cathy and Linton meet on the moors, and it is clear that Linton's health is failing.
- Cathy and Nelly are astonished and alarmed at his ill health. Linton is clearly unable to enjoy the meeting but begs Cathy to stay, and also to report to her father that she has found him in tolerable health.
- Linton is exhausted by the interchange and falls asleep.
- When he awakens he is confused and beset by voices, primarily his father's, which torment him.
- Following Nelly's inclination, they foolishly decide to keep from Edgar the extent of his nephew's ill health.

ANALYSIS

READING THE SIGNS

In this chapter we are again confronted with a **narrator** who is unable or unwilling to read the signs. Nelly perceives that Linton is seriously enfeebled but permits neither herself nor Edgar that knowledge. This reluctance to acknowledge Linton's illness has disastrous consequences for Cathy. Nelly's refusal to acknowledge the gravity of Linton's illness exactly reiterates her earlier fatal failure to acknowledge Catherine's malady.

CRITICAL VIEWPOINT A03

In this chapter we could argue that illness is not so much used as a strategy but rather impedes the trajectory of Heathcliff's plot.

STUDY FOCUS: DREAMS   A02

While he is asleep on the moors, Linton dreams that his father is calling for him and awakes in terror, 'under the spell of the imaginary voice' (p. 263). This reiterates Brontë's use of the dream world to comment on the real world. What should be a tender love scene between the two cousins is fractured and disturbed by Linton's dream.

VOLUME II, CHAPTER XIII

SUMMARY

- Cathy and Nelly repeat their meeting with Linton on the moors. This meeting, like the last, is fraught with conflict.
- Linton acts as a decoy to get Cathy and Nelly back to the Heights.
- Cathy knows that she is being manipulated by Linton, but she does not understand why.
- Linton's terror of Heathcliff is manifest, and when Heathcliff appears on the scene he is remorselessly angry with Linton.
- Heathcliff reveals that he only cares that Linton should outlive Edgar.
- Cathy and Nelly are kept prisoner at Wuthering Heights.
- Once back at the Heights, Linton visibly improves and it is clear that his part in the plan has succeeded.
- Cathy bites and scratches Heathcliff in her attempt to wrest the keys from him, and his response is to beat her thoroughly, much to Nelly's indignation.
- Heathcliff's plan is that the two cousins should marry in the morning.
- Cathy pleads with Heathcliff to be permitted to return to the Grange and promises to marry Linton in return, but Heathcliff refuses her request and tells her that her father must die alone.

ANALYSIS

A FAIRY-TALE WORLD?

This chapter contains many of the major themes of the novel: deceit, revenge, marriage, imprisonment and violence. Imprisoned at the Heights, Nelly and Catherine miss their chance of escape when three servants from the Grange come seeking them, and they are kept captive for the next four days. At this point the novel appears to recall its fairy-tale status and rehearses some of the structures of traditional fairy tales such as 'Beauty and the Beast', thus re-emphasising the oppressive nature of the marriage contract for women in the nineteenth century. Nelly reveals her legal and clerical knowledge when she reminds Heathcliff that his crime is 'felony without benefit of clergy' (p. 274).

It is worth noting that Cathy's response to the imprisonment is a reaction first of passion and resolve and then of appeal. She bites and scratches. Heathcliff retaliates with an equally violent response, slapping her about the head. She then appeals to Heathcliff to let Nelly go and inform her father, so that he may not die alone and wondering where she is: 'Mr Heathcliff, you're a cruel man, but you're not a fiend' (p. 275). The pattern of this response can be seen as being broadly allied to the two houses: a fierce reaction appropriate to the Heights, and a gentle one, more in keeping with the rules of conduct at the Grange. This is a neat demonstration of the fact that Cathy embodies both qualities and can draw on them equally.

STUDY FOCUS: THE ROLE OF LANDSCAPE | A02

At the beginning of the chapter Brontë describes 'a golden afternoon of August – every breath from the hills so full of life, that it seemed whoever respired it, though dying, might revive' (pp. 265–6). This is both symbolic and ironic. Brontë never gives us merely a literal description of the landscape. Usually such descriptions are symbolic, reflecting mood or character, using the technique called **pathetic fallacy**. Here the afternoon itself is deceiving: the hills, so full of life, first witness Linton's dramatised illness and then are the site of Cathy and Nelly's betrayal, which Cathy fears will result in her father's lonely death.

CHECK THE BOOK | A03

Angela Carter's collection of **Gothic**-inspired fairy tales, *The Bloody Chamber*, explores many of these themes. See 'The Bloody Chamber' and 'The Tiger's Bride' for retellings of 'Beauty and the Beast'. In the former, which is also related to the 'Bluebeard' story, the unnamed heroine escapes from her husband's castle with the help of her mother.

CONTEXT | A04

Nelly's reference is to the system of laws which exempt clergy from civil prosecution for certain crimes. Her point here is that Heathcliff's crime is so heinous that there will be no escape clause to which he might appeal for mercy.

GLOSSARY

266 **bespeak** beg for
267 **ling** heather
275 **eft** small lizard-like animal

VOLUME II, CHAPTER XIV

SUMMARY

- On the fifth day Nelly is able to return to the Grange where Edgar is barely alive.
- Meanwhile, Cathy is married to Linton.
- Nelly informs Edgar of Heathcliff's plan and Edgar decides to change his will.
- The lawyer, bribed by Heathcliff to ignore Edgar Linton's summons, arrives too late, but Cathy arrives back just in time to witness her father's dying moments.

ANALYSIS

INHERITANCE

The complex inheritance laws of the nineteenth century are here shown to be absolutely integral to the plot. It can be argued that *Wuthering Heights* has a profoundly **feminist** agenda, since although the female characters all have power to a greater or lesser extent, they are all disempowered by the social structures of marriage, motherhood and inheritance. Since Edgar Linton fails to change his will and tie up his property in trusts, Linton is correct in his odious assumption that all Cathy's property now belongs to him (p. 280).

CHECK THE BOOK A03

Miriam Allott's essay 'The Rejection of Heathcliff' (1958), in her book of critical essays on *Wuthering Heights*, is a careful analysis of our shifting responses to Heathcliff's villainy.

STUDY FOCUS: A DIFFERENT VIEW OF HEATHCLIFF? A02

This second volume appears to be all to do with revenge, rather than love. Our attention is once more with Heathcliff as he imprisons Cathy, insists upon her marriage to Linton and prevents her from going to her dying father. Yet these terrible acts lack the passion of his behaviour in the earlier part of the novel. It is worth considering how Brontë retains our sympathy for Heathcliff in the light of these deeds in Volume II. Largely, our response to Heathcliff is constantly adjusted and refined by our responses to the other characters: the pity we feel for Cathy and Nelly, the disgust we feel for the self-centred Linton and the complicated reaction we have to Hareton, who loves Heathcliff.

VOLUME II, CHAPTER XV

SUMMARY

- After the funeral of her father, Cathy remains at the Grange with Nelly.
- Heathcliff arrives and, as master of the property, demands that Cathy return to the Heights, outlining his intentions to put a tenant in the Grange.
- He reveals his plans to be buried in the same space as Catherine, and tells Nelly how Catherine has haunted him over the years.
- He returns to the Heights with Cathy, leaving Nelly alone at the Grange.

ANALYSIS

GHOSTS

Heathcliff, when he arrives at the Grange to bring Cathy back to the Heights, significantly describes himself as a 'ghost' (p. 287). As he is telling Nelly how he opened the coffin to see Catherine, and plans to lie next to her and be buried with her so that their bodies will merge long before Edgar Linton's decomposes into them, he makes the confident assertion: 'I have a strong faith in ghosts; I have a conviction that they can, and do exist, among us' (p. 289). Heathcliff's account of Catherine's ghost and how it has haunted him over the years revises for us the absolute and unconsummated passion that marked their relationship while she was alive: he sleeps in her chamber only to be disappointed; he 'ought to have sweat blood then, from the anguish of [his] yearning' (p. 290).

> **GRADE BOOSTER** A02
>
> The ghost of Catherine that Heathcliff summons, while disturbing, has as real a feel as any of the characters, and Brontë encourages us to believe in its reality. Even Nelly does not gainsay Heathcliff here. It is worth contrasting her reaction to Heathcliff's account of Catherine's ghost to her reaction to Catherine's attempt to tell her of her dreams in Volume I, Chapter IX.

STUDY FOCUS: A TRANSGRESSIVE LOVE   A03

Critical attention has focused on the transgressive nature of this chapter. Certainly, Heathcliff's description of his plan to merge with Catherine is grisly, and equally it is a plan which transgresses the boundary between life and death, and between propriety and necrophilia. As Nancy Armstrong observes in her essay 'Brontë in and out of her Time'(in Patsy Stoneman (ed.), *Wuthering Heights: Contemporary Critical Essays*, 1993), Heathcliff's plan can be interpreted as an occult dramatisation of a demonic love which utterly defies the conventions of nineteenth-century romance. This highlights a further **Gothic** strand to the novel, and connects it to the later work *Dracula* where Bram Stoker further blurs the boundaries between life and death, and desire, with his eponymous 'undead' vampire.

VOLUME II, CHAPTER XVI

SUMMARY

- Linton dies, and Cathy is too proud to accept offers of friendship from either Hareton or Zillah, so she remains isolated at the Heights.
- Nelly Dean's story ends here, with her unable to foresee any kind of future for Cathy unless she is able to remarry.
- The narrative passes back to Lockwood, who reveals his intention to give up his tenancy of the Grange in October.

ANALYSIS

NARRATIVE STRUCTURE

At the beginning of this chapter, Nelly tells the story in the person of Zillah, the housekeeper at the Heights. A structural analysis of this device might focus on the ways in which narratives are contained within each other, for the whole of the story is Lockwood's, which encompasses Nelly's, and now Zillah's.

INHERITANCE

Since Linton is a minor when he dies, he cannot leave the property that he inherits by marrying Cathy to his father, but Heathcliff claims a right to it in any case. Cathy's position as a dispossessed widow radically disables her from contesting Heathcliff's command of the property and land.

CHECK THE BOOK **A04**

See Emily Brontë's 1841 poem 'I do not weep, I would not weep', which refers to the comfort derived from a belief in the afterlife.

STUDY FOCUS: THE POWER OF DEATH **A02**

Cathy's response to Linton's death is that she feels dead herself: 'He's safe, and I'm free … but … You have left me so long to struggle against death, alone, that I feel and see only death! I feel like death!' (p. 294). This response seems to be in marked contrast to Brontë's typical response to death, which does not diminish love in any way. This suggests that for all she professes to have loved Linton, the love she felt for him was weak and inauthentic. This is in stark contrast to how both Edgar and Heathcliff respond to Catherine's death.

CATHY AND HARETON

After Linton's death, Cathy stays in her room for a fortnight but finally comes down to join the rest of the household, where she sits by the fire and reads. Hareton is entranced, both by her curls and by her reading, and asks her to read to them, a request which she angrily refuses, mistaking it for a pretence of kindness. Once again, we see Brontë setting up the relationship between her characters through misunderstanding and misreading.

GLOSSARY

292	**thrang**	busy
294	**fain**	glad
295	**train-oil**	whale-oil (for cleaning guns)
295	**that road**	in that direction, as far as that is concerned
296	**starved**	chilled
296	**taking**	rage
297	**stalled of**	tired of

VOLUME II, CHAPTER XVII

SUMMARY

- The narrative returns to Lockwood and the present day.
- Lockwood takes a note to Cathy from Nelly, and reveals to Heathcliff that he has come to terminate his tenancy.

ANALYSIS

LOCKWOOD

With the resumption of the narratorial position, Lockwood brings the **narrative** back to the present day. He agrees to take a note from Nelly to Cathy at the Heights, where once again he is rudely received by both Hareton and Cathy. Structurally, this mirrors the first chapter and completes the double arc of the narratives. Lockwood's clumsy attempt to pass Nelly's note secretly to Cathy is thwarted by her assumption that it is a love note. When she eventually learns that Nelly is the real author of the letter she is filled with reminiscent longing.

The chapter ends with Lockwood's self-conceited reflection:

> What a realization of something more romantic than a fairy tale it would have been for Mrs Linton Heathcliff, had she and I struck up an attachment, as her good nurse desired, and migrated together, into the stirring atmosphere of the town! (p. 304)

READING

This chapter brings into focus once more Brontë's views on education, and on reading in particular. Once again, reading and misreading notes, books and situations becomes a way of establishing character and also moving the action forward. Having lost her opportunity to read Nelly's note, Cathy continues to scorn Hareton's attempts to improve his education. Hareton's response to this is a violent mix of 'mortification and wrath' (p. 302) which manifests itself as 'a manual check' (a slap on the face which splits her lip, p. 303), and eventually, in distress, he throws all his books upon the fire. Brontë here reiterates the tensions and difficulties of acquiring valuable knowledge: Cathy jettisons her chance, and Hareton likewise jettisons his own, much to their individual distress.

STUDY FOCUS: LOCKWOOD'S DEFERRAL (A03)

Lockwood's deferral of real relationships in favour of the romantic dream have already been commented upon from the first chapter where he reports his holiday infatuation with his 'goddess'. He can only contemplate the (fairy-tale) relationship with Cathy once it is clear to him that this is an impossibility. As Margaret Homans notes in her **feminist** reading of the novel: 'Lockwood's … entire narrative is predicated on romantic desires, endless oscillations of approach and avoidance' (Linda H. Peterson (ed.), *Wuthering Heights: Case Studies in Contemporary Criticism*, 1992, p. 345).

GLOSSARY

301 **Chevy Chase** a medieval English ballad

303 **causeway** a cobbled area, pavement

VOLUME II, CHAPTER XVIII

SUMMARY

- 1802. Lockwood happens to be in the locality again and is seized by the impulse to visit the Grange.
- He also visits the Heights where, peeping through the window, a picture of domestic bliss greets him.
- Cathy teaches Hareton to read.
- Nelly Dean receives Lockwood warmly and tells him that Heathcliff died three months earlier, a death which she describes as a '"queer" end' (p. 309).

ANALYSIS

EDUCATION

The narration now passes back to Nelly, and she describes for Lockwood the developing relationship between Hareton and Cathy. The relationship has been conducted around learning, both in terms of Hareton's acquisition of literacy skills, and Cathy's developing humility.

Critics have tended to see this relationship between Cathy and Hareton as the resolution of all the conflicts of the novel, though opinion is divided as to whether the relationship constitutes a successful resolution.

STUDY FOCUS: THE IMAGERY OF AN ENDING A02

The descriptions of the landscape are full of light: the glow of the sinking sun (p. 307) the 'mild glory of a rising moon' (p. 307), a 'beamless, amber light along the west' (p. 307). This use of light is symbolic, as Brontë sheds light on the resolution of the conflicts and struggles of the preceding chapters.

GLOSSARY		
305	**frough**	from
305	**wick**	week
306	**mensful**	decent
308	**haulf**	half
308	**sartin**	certain
309	**fellies**	male admirers
309	**jocks**	jugs
313	**side out of t' gait**	get out of the way
315	**Aw's gang**	I'm going
315	**it 'ull be mitch**	you'll be lucky

VOLUME II, CHAPTER XIX

SUMMARY

- The narrative time moves backwards to before Heathcliff's death.
- Cathy and Hareton begin to negotiate their relationship under the hostile eyes of Joseph and Heathcliff.
- Heathcliff's will for revenge has diminished now that it lies within his power.
- Heathcliff desires to die in order to be reunited with Catherine, but feels himself to be trapped within a healthy body.

ANALYSIS

CATHY AND HARETON

Nelly recommences her narrative with a description of how Hareton and Cathy begin to form their friendship, and the implications that their friendship has for the political structure of the household. An anecdote about them digging up Joseph's prized blackcurrant bushes in order to plant flowers is indicative of Cathy's will to cultivate the garden and transform the Heights from a utilitarian place into a place for pleasure. Readings of the novel which see Cathy's relationship with Hareton as the resolution of the conflict between the two houses might wish to explore the planting of flowers as the integration of nature and culture implied in the term 'cultivation'. The flowers are described as an 'importation of plants from the Grange' (p. 317) and thus are suggestive of Cathy's own position, scion of Catherine, imported from the Grange to her truly native soil. That she is displacing Joseph's blackcurrant bushes is indicative of the fact that his way of life must now give way to a new generation.

Similarly, she sticks primroses into Hareton's porridge (p. 318), a sign of frivolity and decoration which moves the plain functionality of the meal into a new and celebratory dimension.

HEATHCLIFF

Her newfound friendship with Hareton gives Cathy the confidence to rebel against Heathcliff's tyranny. It is significant that this is the moment when Heathcliff's deceit might be exposed, but the love Hareton has for him stills his hand and Cathy's tongue. However, Heathcliff has abandoned his plans for revenge and now only wishes to die. The whole world seems to be constructed of memorabilia of Catherine, and Heathcliff feels trapped in a body which refuses to die, whereas his soul is already 'in the torments of hell' (p. 161). The rhetoric of this quotation has its origins in Emily Brontë's poetry.

STUDY FOCUS: MEMORABILIA (A03)

J. Hillis Miller's deconstructive reading of the novel (*Fiction and Repetition*, 1982) particularly focuses attention on the emphasis in this chapter upon memorabilia. He argues that each thing that Heathcliff encounters reminds him not of Catherine, but of his loss of Catherine. Like all texts, the memoranda alert us to the loss of the thing they remind us of, and not to its presence. Hillis Miller is drawing our attention to the reality gap between the world of the text and the real world. The world Brontë draws seems real but actually depicts only what is lost (not really present). Heathcliff treasures each thing that reminds him of Catherine, but despises it in equal measure because it sharpens his despair at having lost her.

CRITICAL VIEWPOINT (A03)

It could be argued that under Nelly's maternal eye the Heights has been transformed into a place of sunshine and relative peace. The house is no longer barred and gated. Its boundaries have been opened up.

GLOSSARY

318 **lug** carry

319 **yah muh bend tuh th' yoak** you may bend to the yoke; i.e. you can put up with her ways

319 **een** eyes

323 **mattock** garden implement

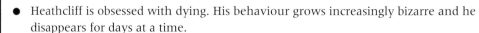

VOLUME II, CHAPTER XX

SUMMARY

- Heathcliff is obsessed with dying. His behaviour grows increasingly bizarre and he disappears for days at a time.
- When he returns, it is in a glittery, strangely joyful mood. His manner quite discomfits Nelly, who is superstitious about ghosts and the inexplicable.
- Nelly tries to convince him to make a will, and to repent of his former ways and turn to God.
- Two days later he dies, threatening Nelly that if she does not bury his body according to his wishes he will haunt her forever.
- Hareton, who has been the most wronged by Heathcliff, is the only person who really mourns his loss.
- Heathcliff is buried according to his desires, against the opened side of Catherine's coffin.
- Local legend has it that their ghosts still walk the moors.

ANALYSIS

A GHOSTLY WORLD

The last chapter again revisits the conflict between ethical convention and a higher morality associated with passion. Nelly wonders whether Heathcliff is a 'ghoul, or a vampire' (p. 330) and ponders again his uncertain beginnings. With no provenance, no real kinship to any of the other characters, Heathcliff becomes both like a ghost and vampiric – feeding upon the lives of ordinary people.

Almost at the end of the novel a small child, with a sheep and two lambs, encounters the ghosts of Heathcliff and Catherine as he is walking along the Nab (p. 336). This is a neutral outsider commenting on the ghosts. He is a child, he guides the lamb. These associations are all signs of his 'innocence' and therefore his 'credibility' within the story. We must believe in ghosts, according to Brontë, for they have been seen walking among us.

STUDY FOCUS: LOCKWOOD'S LAST WORDS | A02

Lockwood hears the end of the story, and on walking past the graveyard on his way home pauses to wonder 'how any one could ever imagine unquiet slumbers, for the sleepers in that quiet earth' (p. 337). This reveals not only Lockwood's peculiar lack of imagination, but also his continued inability to comprehend the signs of the landscape in which he moves. Lockwood's continued incompetence as a reader of signs throws into disarray all his assumptions as **narrator** throughout the novel, causing us to reconsider his judgements.

CONTEXT | A04

Brontë once again asserts a profound disconnect between her version of heaven and the conventional Victorian view in this chapter: 'I have nearly attained *my* heaven; and that of others is altogether unvalued, and uncoveted by me' (p. 333). This was a radical statement to make in fiction at a time when Christian religion was at the heart of social values.

GLOSSARY

328 **rare and pleased** highly delighted

334 **chuck** a term of endearment

335 **girnning** grinning or grimacing: the rictus smile of death

CHARACTERS

CHARACTERISATION

Of all forms of literature, novels are particularly compelling because they seduce us into believing that in reading we are expanding our knowledge of people and life. Of course, readers know that characters are not real people, yet it is difficult to follow any novel if one constantly reminds oneself that the characters are merely literary constructs. Indeed, one of the primary ways in which we might judge a novel is in terms of whether or not we care sufficiently about its characters. In *Wuthering Heights* Brontë offers us an intriguing array of characters.

It is conventional to consider characterisation in terms of identity. What characterises this person? How are they identified? One of the key elements of identity might be thought to be a character's name, yet *Wuthering Heights* is a novel in which there scarcely seem enough names to go round. There is a constant doubling of names that occur and recur through the three generations of the novel.

It is worth paying attention to the ways in which Brontë introduces her characters. From the first chapter we see Lockwood through his diary entry. We get an impression of him through his language, not a physical description. Similarly, when we meet Joseph, our impression of him is formed through his speech, his language. The first thing Joseph says is simple and biblical – 'The Lord help us!' (p. 4) – and then we immediately hear his colloquial, mumbling, almost unintelligible dialect. There is a minimum of physical description, and this contributes to an emphasis on emotion. We may not understand Joseph, but we learn to 'read' his emotional character very quickly.

Brontë constructs her characters with great economy. Her characterisation is rarely permitted to interrupt the pace of the story. Equally tantalisingly, Brontë plays with our expectations of characters as separate and coherent individuals. They extend their influence beyond the grave; they share each other's names and moods; and they exemplify all manner of contradictions.

CHECK THE BOOK **A04**

Nicholas Marsh (*Emily Bronte: Wuthering Heights*, Analysing Texts series, 1999) gives a full and interesting analysis of Brontë's characterisation.

CATHERINE

WHO IS CATHERINE?

- Catherine is born Catherine Earnshaw and grows up at Wuthering Heights.
- She marries Edgar Linton but passionately loves Heathcliff.
- Catherine dies after the birth of her daughter, Catherine Linton.

GHOSTLY CATHERINE

The reader's first introduction to Catherine Earnshaw is an introduction to the signature of a ghost: her name is scratched upon the window ledge in her childhood bedroom, the room where Lockwood will have his disturbing nightmares. We cannot avoid the figure of Catherine, as it is carved into the very text. At the end of the novel, Heathcliff is tormented by everything that signals to him his loss of Catherine. She is as elusive and forbidden to him as she is incomprehensible to Lockwood.

A SPLIT IDENTITY

The names which Lockwood finds inscribed upon the window – Catherine Earnshaw, Catherine Linton, Catherine Heathcliff – can be read as indicative of Catherine's fractured or fragmented social identity. She struggles with conflicting ideas of herself as she tries to combine two irreconcilable lives: the life of passion fully experienced, and the life of social convention that secures her to either her father or her husband.

STUDY FOCUS: CULTURE VERSUS NATURE (A02)

The conflict that disturbs Catherine's sense of self is played out in the novel through the theme of culture versus nature. In deciding to marry Edgar Linton, Catherine chooses culture over nature. This is directly contrasted with a narrative insistence upon her love of nature and her oneness with nature. As a child, for example, rather than read, she and Heathcliff prefer to scramble on the moors. Her diary, which documents the fact, pays scrupulous attention to her jettisoning of the book but neglects to describe her impression of the moors. From Catherine's perspective, nature does not need to be named and it does not lend itself to narrative representation or to culture. If we accept this reading, then Catherine's choice of Edgar over Heathcliff cannot be expected to be successful.

KEY QUOTATIONS: CATHERINE (A01)

Key quotation 1:

Nelly Dean's first introduction of Catherine is as 'mischievous and wayward' (p. 38).

Possible interpretations:

- We can expect Catherine to make unpredictable and surprising choices.
- Catherine is capable of great love and fidelity, but is equally capable of ruthless destruction, involving her own death and bringing wretched misery to those she loves.

Key quotation 2:

To Nelly Dean: ' "I *am* Heathcliff" ' (p. 82).

Possible interpretations:

- Catherine's assertion is both dramatic and memorable, and shows her great passion.
- It shows her unstable sense of identity which cannot be stabilised by Heathcliff as he too is enigmatic and uncertain.

CRITICAL VIEWPOINT (A03)

Characterisation of Catherine starts and ends in an enigma: the world of the novel is testament to her character, but it is testament to a character that can leave only the ghostly signs of itself behind.

GRADE BOOSTER (A02)

AO2 explores how a writer's narrative decisions shape meaning. In relation to Catherine, you could gain marks by showing that her identity is shaped by Brontë in her portrayal of Catherine's shifting social relationships.

HEATHCLIFF

WHO IS HEATHCLIFF?

- Heathcliff is a foundling who is brought home by Mr Earnshaw from a trip to Liverpool, and is named after a dead son.
- He is passionately in love with Catherine, but forms no other attachments.
- He marries Isabella Linton and together they have a son, Linton Heathcliff.
- He dies longing to be reunited with Catherine.

HEATHCLIFF THE OUTSIDER

Unlike every other character in the novel, Heathcliff has only a singular name that serves him as both Christian name and surname. This places him radically outside social patterns and conventions. Heathcliff belongs first nowhere and finally anywhere. The fact that he inherits his name from a dead son also signals the potential for belonging and invention, since this name might then be thought of as that of a ghost: a character who is no longer present.

MONSTER OR HERO?

As a foundling, Heathcliff is introduced into the close-knit family structure as an outsider; he is perceived as both gift and threat, and these conflicting identifications form part of the compelling undecidability of his character. Contradiction typifies Heathcliff. To Catherine he is brother and lover; to Isabella he is romantic hero and pitiless oppressor. He epitomises potency, yet he fathers an exceptionally frail child. He encompasses vast philosophical opposites: love and death, culture and nature, evil and heroism. Some critics, most notably Clifton Snider, have focused on the supernatural qualities of this novel to read Heathcliff as vampiric. Whether we read Heathcliff as monstrous or as a **Byronic hero**, he disturbs the conventional structure of the novel, and of the world created within it.

STUDY FOCUS: A BYRONIC HERO (A02)

Critics have most often cited Heathcliff as a Byronic hero: powerful, attractive, melancholy and brutal. Through most of the first volume of the novel Heathcliff's rise to power details the ascension of the **Romantic** hero, with his intrusion into and transformation of a conventional and socially limited world. However, by making such romantic conventions manifest in an energetic new form, Heathcliff actually cancels out Romantic possibilities and reduces that system to mere superstition. Thus in creating Heathcliff, Brontë may well have been acknowledging Byron's influence. But in the character of Catherine she also suggests a revision of Byron and demonstrates his vision as a fundamentally male literary myth.

KEY QUOTATIONS: HEATHCLIFF (A01)

Key quotation 1:
Heathcliff is described by Catherine as an 'unreclaimed creature' (p. 102).
Possible interpretations:
- He does not belong in, nor can he be claimed by, any social structure such as the family.
- He has a mysterious capacity for self-invention, which defies the conventional categories of characterisation in the novel.
- He is profoundly difficult to read for most of the other characters.

Key quotation 2:
Catherine warning Isabella about Heathcliff says: '"He's not a rough diamond – a pearl-containing oyster of a rustic; he's a fierce, pitiless, wolfish man"' (p.103).
Possible interpretations:
- We can expect great cruelty from Heathcliff towards Isabella.
- He is uncivilised, and even love will not tame him. The fact that this assessment comes from Catherine, who loves him, means that we treat it very seriously.

CRITICAL VIEWPOINT (A03)

When we meet Heathcliff as a child, the things we find out about him are that he is capable of enduring anything (p. 38) and that he has a profound connection with Catherine. These two characteristics remain with him throughout the novel, and are what enable him to achieve his ends.

CONTEXT (A04)

The description 'Byronic' means characteristic of or resembling Byron or his poetry: that is, contemptuous of and rebelling against conventional morality. Lord Byron (1788–1824), the most flamboyant and notorious of the Romantic poets, created the idea of the Romantic hero: unruly, melancholy and haunted by secret guilt.

EDGAR

WHO IS EDGAR?

● Edgar is Edgar Linton, heir to Thrushcross Grange.

● He loves, and marries, Catherine Earnshaw, and together they have a child, Catherine Linton.

● Edgar is brother to Isabella.

EDGAR THE BOY

Edgar's world is an interior world, and we first see him as a child, poetically pictured by Heathcliff for Nelly Dean. Edgar's world is: 'a splendid place carpeted with crimson, and crimson-covered chairs and tables, and a pure white ceiling bordered by gold, a shower of glass-drops hanging in silver chains from the centre and shimmering with little soft tapers' (p. 48). In the midst of this sumptuous environment, the description of which sits so uncomfortably in Heathcliff's mouth, stands Edgar, weeping by the fire. And Heathcliff despises him for his pettiness. From our first introduction to Edgar we perceive him to be emotional and a 'petted thing' (p. 48).

EDGAR THE MAN

CRITICAL VIEWPOINT A03

The descriptions of Edgar as a 'spoiled child', a 'soft thing' and 'a lamb [who] threatens like a bull' (p. 114) establish him as artificial in contrast to the elemental descriptions afforded Heathcliff and Catherine. And yet, although there is no way that Edgar the man can satisfy Catherine, he nevertheless loves her in a conventional way as his wife, and when she is ill he tends her devotedly.

As a man, Edgar Linton is described as lacking spirit, and this can be read in two ways. Conventionally, he does lack the vigour that characterises Catherine and Heathcliff. However, he also lacks their ghostliness, the spectral quality which sets them apart and lends them mystery. By comparison, Edgar's corporeality is easy to read. He is not troubled by internal contradiction, and he remains in his place throughout the novel, living at Thrushcross Grange as boy and man, and finally resting in his grave alongside the body of his wife.

STUDY FOCUS: MASCULINE OR FEMININE? A02

It is rather a commonplace of criticism to read Edgar as effeminate, in contrast to the savage masculinity of Heathcliff. The **feminist** critics Gilbert and Gubar (*The Madwoman in the Attic: The Woman Writer and the Nineteenth-Century Literary Imagination*, 1979) have reversed this trend, reading Edgar as masculine and Heathcliff as feminine. Edgar's masculinity, they argue, is that of social power. He legitimately inherits Thrushcross Grange; his books and his library establish him as a man of letters and therefore of influence. Nelly's constant reference to Edgar as 'the master' reveals her opinion of him as someone with social power.

KEY QUOTATIONS: EDGAR A01

Key quotation 1:

Nelly, consoling Heathcliff, says: '"Edgar Linton shall look quite a doll beside you"' (p. 57).

Possible interpretations:

● We are encouraged to see Edgar as a plaything, not someone who plays. He has no agency.

● In comparison to Heathcliff, Edgar is frail and easily discarded.

Key quotation 2:

Catherine's description of Edgar: '"Your type is not a lamb, it's a sucking leveret"' (p. 115).

Possible interpretations:

● Edgar is weaker than a lamb. As an unweaned hare, he would be prey to every predator.

● Edgar is in need of love. It is significant that this outburst comes in the middle of an argument between Edgar, Heathcliff and Catherine.

ISABELLA

WHO IS ISABELLA?

- Isabella is Edgar Linton's sister.
- She falls in love with and marries Heathcliff, much against Catherine and Edgar's advice.
- Edgar disowns her and Heathcliff treats her cruelly.
- Realising her mistake, she flees Heathcliff and goes down south for the rest of her life.
- While in the south of England she bears Heathcliff's son, Linton Heathcliff.
- Isabella dies when Linton is twelve years old.

VIXEN OR CANARY?

Isabella is frequently referred to with animal imagery. In Volume I, Chapter X, she is likened to a monkey, a little canary, a sparrow's egg, a cat, a tigress, a vixen and a dove. These characteristics serve to demonstrate her complex nature, a mixture of helplessness and ferocity. Ultimately, she will be destroyed by the forces which range against her, but given the insistence upon the animal imagery throughout her characterisation, we are encouraged to read this as part of nature, and a natural consequence of her personality and the choices she makes.

CONTEXT A04

Darwin's *The Origin of Species*, which outlines his theory of evolution and the survival of the fittest, was a key work in the nineteenth century.

STUDY FOCUS: IS ISABELLA HER OWN CHARACTER? A03

As she is Edgar's sister, Isabella's characterisation is closely associated with his. Indeed, she is only ever seen in relation to other characters. Isabella's attachment to Heathcliff, which structurally parallels Edgar's fascination with Catherine, fails to develop into a mature and unselfish love. Her infatuation with Heathcliff is a direct result of her cultural life: she can only read Heathcliff as a **Romantic** hero, and she never entirely abandons her fantasy of Heathcliff as the Byronic lover, even when it is clear that his spontaneous love of Catherine has transformed itself into a determined lust for revenge, for which Isabella is only a cipher or vehicle. Feminist critics, looking at the novel from the perspective of **gynocriticism**, have devoted their attention to the brutal realities of Isabella's position as a battered wife, and have theorised the power relations that seem to make her complicit in her oppression.

CHECK THE BOOK A03

See Mills et al., *Feminist Readings, Feminists Reading* (1989), for a provocative and wide-ranging collection of essays from a number of feminist positions.

KEY QUOTATION: ISABELLA A01

Key quotation:

Catherine describes Isabella to Nelly Dean noting '"the brightness of Isabella's yellow hair, and the whiteness of her skin … her dainty elegance, and the fondness all the family exhibit for her"' (p. 98).

Possible interpretations:

- This description is significantly inanimate. Isabella appears like a portrait of herself, or a doll, not a person.
- There are similar descriptions of Edgar. This account of the Lintons emphasises their civility and status.

LINTON

WHO IS LINTON?

- Linton Heathcliff is the son of Isabella Linton and Heathcliff.
- He is Cathy's first cousin.
- For the first twelve years of his life he lives in the south of England but comes back to Yorkshire when his mother dies.
- Edgar Linton wishes to look after him at the Grange, but Heathcliff prevails and Linton is sent up to the Heights to live.
- Linton and Cathy marry, in spite of Linton's ill health.

CONFLICTING IDENTITY

Linton Heathcliff is a contradiction in terms. His name signifies the unnatural union between Heathcliff and the Lintons, or between passion and convention, and his sickly nature demonstrates the impossibility of such a union. In Linton, love and convention emerge as corrupted by each other. Like both his parents, however, Linton's view of the world is singular, and it is his inability to see it in any but his own terms which renders him absolutely available for manipulation by Heathcliff.

STUDY FOCUS: READING LINTON AS FEMALE A04

It is possible, following Gilbert and Gubar (*The Madwoman in the Attic: The Woman Writer and the Nineteenth-Century Literary Imagination*, 1979), to read Linton as an example of the gender ambiguity with which Brontë imbues her characters. Linton displays many of the characteristics that a Victorian readership would be used to associating with typically female characters: he is manipulative, fickle, sickly, babyish – 'sucking a stick of sugar-candy' (p. 279) – and enfeebled in his relationship to dominant characters.

KEY QUOTATION: LINTON A01

Key quotation:

Brontë reserves for Linton her most scathing imagery: he is described as 'a pet', a 'puling chicken' and a 'whelp' (pp. 199, 207, 208).

Possible interpretation:

- The animal imagery establishes Linton Heathcliff as both immature and less than human.

HARETON

WHO IS HARETON?

- Hareton Earnshaw is the son of Hindley and Frances Earnshaw.
- He is left to run wild, ill-educated and ill-treated.
- He is cousin to Cathy Linton.
- At the end of the book, he and Cathy are planning to marry.

CRITICAL VIEWPOINT A03

Critics are divided as to the usefulness of historical context for an understanding of *Wuthering Heights*. Some critics think that texts are best looked at in isolation, or even that their meanings are created by readers rather than historical factors. Some, like Terry Eagleton, Arnold Kettle and Nancy Armstrong, have focused acute critical attention upon the economic and social conditions which inform the novel, seeing the novel as both a product of and participant in the social context.

LOVE

Hareton's relationship with Cathy has been read as mirroring Heathcliff's with Catherine, in as much as he is desirous of impressing her, and he is proud in her presence. His love of Cathy, however, might be said more closely to resemble Edgar's love of Catherine, in as much as it is moderate yet tender, devoted yet restrained. Hareton also exhibits an unwavering love for Heathcliff, in spite of the ill-treatment he has received at his hands. Like Catherine, Hareton is constant in his initial affections, and when Heathcliff first arrives in his life they form an alliance against Hindley. That Hareton resembles Catherine physically also complicates Heathcliff's relationship with him. Heathcliff loves Hareton in spite of himself, saving his life as a baby and, at the end of the novel, relinquishing all that he has to him.

STUDY FOCUS: INHERITANCE A02

Although Hareton's name is inscribed above the door of Wuthering Heights, his inability to read, coupled with the repetitious doubling of names and signatures, means that he fails to inherit his rightful property. The structural doubling of names means that there is no guarantee of inheritance. Inheritance requires a stable system of patriarchal legitimacy and uncontested identity. Hareton is dispossessed by Heathcliff, but can also be seen as a rewriting of Heathcliff: a surrogate or symbolic Heathcliff. He is finally able to repossess the Heights, only to be immediately assimilated into the cultural **hegemony**, or authority, of the Grange.

EDUCATION

The development of Hareton's characterisation revolves around his education. He is initially nursed by Nelly, the novel's surrogate mother, and under her tuition he begins to learn his letters. However, left to the ministrations of his dissolute and unpredictable father, Hindley, Hareton grows wild and uncultivated, unable to read, and with no social skills. His attempts at self-improvement are a source of mockery and derision for Linton and Cathy, and it is not until the end of the novel that he is able to acquire the skills necessary for him to achieve social equality with Cathy and come into his rightful inheritance. He is taught these skills not without some diminution of his sexual potency, as he sits meekly to be alternately kissed or chastised as he learns. The domestic romance which typifies the final union between Cathy and Hareton may well resolve some of the conflicts that thwart the other relationships in the novel, but their union lacks the grand passion, the wild power of the original love between Catherine and Heathcliff.

KEY QUOTATION: HARETON A01

Key quotation:

Cathy kisses Hareton and makes him a present of a book, and 'He trembled, and his face glowed – all his rudeness, and all his surly harshness had deserted him' (p. 314).

Possible interpretations:

- This is an example of how Brontë uses the synthesis of nature and culture, passion and civilisation to resolve the conflicts of the novel. The instinctive kiss and the accompanying gift ennoble Hareton, and prompt the reconciliation between Cathy and himself.
- It is significant that the romance of the magic kiss is, by itself, insufficient to redeem Hareton. Before the two houses can achieve harmony, he must accept the gift of the book.

CRITICAL VIEWPOINT A03

Among those of his generation, Hareton's character is perhaps the most intriguing, reversing the comparative lack of interest we feel for his father, Hindley. Hareton is brutalised by Heathcliff, structurally repeating Heathcliff's own suffering at the hands of Hindley. His character resolves many of the contradictions in the novel, combining the qualities of both houses: the energy and spirit of the Heights with the willingness to please and gentleness of the Grange.

CATHY

WHO IS CATHY?

- Cathy Linton is the daughter of Catherine and Edgar Linton.
- She is cousin to Linton Heathcliff and Hareton Earnshaw.
- She is brought up in a protected environment at the Grange until she meets Hareton and discovers the world beyond the Grange.
- She marries Linton Heathcliff, and when he dies she continues to live under Heathcliff's tyranny at the Heights.
- She forms a powerful and redemptive relationship with Hareton and by the end of the book is planning to marry him.

CHECK THE BOOK A04

Elizabeth Gaskell's biography of Charlotte Brontë (1857) makes it very clear that the Brontë sisters struggled with the conflict between being a woman and being a writer.

STUDY FOCUS: CATHY AND CATHERINE   A02

Structurally, the second Cathy can be seen as revising her mother's story. She achieves her identity at the price of her mother's, and Edgar always differentiates her in relation to the first Catherine, whose name he never diminished. Unlike Linton, who has the misfortune of inheriting the worst of both his parents, Cathy appears to have inherited the good from both of hers. Cathy embodies her mother's capacity for fierce attachments, but her relationship with Hareton, which resolves the central conflicts of the novel, lacks the destructive power of Catherine's with Heathcliff.

PROUD BUT LOVING

The novel records Cathy's pride, and her insensitive mockery of Hareton's lack of formal knowledge. The resolution of the novel in which she and Hareton form their attachment is something of a mythical resolution, a romantic conclusion which transcends the central conflicts of the novel to restore a traditional novelistic plot of courtship and marriage. Cathy and Hareton's relationship restores to the novel a version of domestic bliss that was the Victorian ideal, but it is well to bear in mind that Brontë's is a version in which Cathy clearly has the upper hand.

KEY QUOTATION: CATHY   A01

Key quotation:

Cathy is described by Nelly as 'the most winning thing that ever brought sunshine into a desolate house – a real beauty in face – with the Earnshaws' handsome dark eyes, but the Lintons' fair skin and small features, and yellow curling hair. Her spirit was high, though not rough, and qualified by a heart, sensitive and lively to excess in its affections ... her love never fierce; it was deep and tender' (p. 189).

Possible interpretations:

- This character reference from Nelly is considerable, and it influences the way we reflect upon the sour behaviour of Cathy Heathcliff as she presents herself in the first volume of the novel.
- Nelly is here speaking to Lockwood, whom she sees as a possible escape route for Cathy, should he be induced to fall in love with her.

NELLY

WHO IS NELLY?

- Nelly Dean is the second and the dominant narratorial voice in this novel.
- In keeping with her dual roles (narrator and character), she has two names: Nelly, which is used by her peers and familiars, and Ellen, which is used as a mark of respect.
- She is servant to both houses during the course of the novel.
- She acts as a mother figure to most of the characters in the novel, including Lockwood, the other **narrator**.

STUDY FOCUS: NARRATOR AND SERVANT A02

As narrator, Nelly Dean takes up the story from Lockwood and gives it both substance and credence. Lockwood's inability to read the signs of the culture in which he finds himself cannot sustain the story, though it acts to remind us that all narratorial voices, including Nelly's, are partial or biased. As a narrator, she might be read as being the 'servant' of the text, since she brings it to us and provides us with an explicatory commentary. Nelly Dean is a local, and has known each generation of the Earnshaw and Linton families. She is therefore well placed to offer Lockwood a commentary upon the events she describes. Her position as servant is differentiated from that of the other servants, both in terms of the fact that she appears to move effortlessly between the two houses, mediating between their differences, and in terms of her voice. She also emerges as an educated woman, having read most of the books in the library at Thrushcross Grange – the house of culture; she has also experienced the vicissitudes of life at Wuthering Heights – the house of nature.

LANGUAGE AND DIALECT

Nelly Dean is one of the most interesting characters in the novel, not least because of the language she uses. Both **feminist** and **Marxist** critics have acknowledged that in looking at literary texts it is important to consider the way in which women's access to language and education is ideologically determined. Nelly Dean, however, occupies a unique cultural position in this novel. Nelly Dean does not share a regional dialect with the other servants, although she understands it perfectly well. She has access to a range of discourses that might be considered 'beyond her ken' in terms of her position as a family servant; yet as the central narrator, Brontë presents her as a speaking subject, partially excluded from culture but nonetheless positioned so as to be able to comment upon it.

MOTHER FIGURE

Nelly acts as a surrogate mother to many of the motherless characters in this novel: she brings up Hareton for the first five years of his life; she cares for Cathy from birth through to her marriage to Linton; she regrets the brevity of her charge of Linton Heathcliff, which is forced by circumstance; and she acts as confidant and adviser to Catherine and Heathcliff. She also acts as a mother figure to Lockwood as she nurses him back to health. As surrogate mother, Nelly provides food and moral sustenance to her nurslings. Q. D. Leavis, writing in the 1930s, has this to say of Nelly Dean: 'Nelly Dean is most carefully, consistently and convincingly created for us as the normal woman, whose truly feminine nature satisfies itself in nurturing all the children of the book in turn' (reprinted in Stoneman (ed.), *Wuthering Heights: Contemporary Critical Essays*, 1993, p. 28). Contemporary feminist critics may take issue with this conflation of essential feminine nature and maternity, but this was certainly the ideology of the day for Victorian readers.

This reading of Nelly as a mother figure alerts us to another of her roles, for Nelly is a Mother Goose, the teller of this fairy tale, the keeper of its wisdom. The name might also be a corruption of Mother Gossip. Both of these definitions are pertinent to the figure of Nelly, since the knowledge she conveys is at least twofold: it is about women's experience, and it is about the nature of love.

GRADE BOOSTER A02

Being able to identify the different ways in which Nelly uses language will enhance the quality of your essay.

CHECK THE BOOK A04

Marina Warner observes in her analysis of fairy tales that: 'The goose was sacred to the Goddess of Love, Aphrodite' (*From the Beast to the Blonde*, 1994, p. 51).

THEMES

LOVE

Wuthering Heights has been called the greatest of love stories, and the novel's attraction as a love story is not difficult to identify. Indeed, the love story is central to *Wuthering Heights*. This is a novel which explores love from a number of different perspectives: domestic, maternal, social, romantic, religious and **transcendent**. But it is also a novel which explores that theme through a range of conventions which startled and confused its contemporary readership, and it still causes us to reflect on our conventional notions of what constitutes the **genre** of the love story. In the central relationship between Catherine and Heathcliff, Brontë takes the sweep of idealised romance, for example and fuses it with **Gothic** fantasy and horror. In the comfortable domestic realism of Catherine's marriage to Edgar, Brontë interleaves a **theme** of illness and childbirth which eventually leads to death.

Fantasy characterises the relationship between Isabella and Heathcliff, and similarly that between Catherine and Edgar. They love in the other something they cannot achieve for themselves. By contrast, it can be argued that narcissism, i.e. extreme love of oneself, characterises the relationship between Heathcliff and Catherine.

STUDY FOCUS: LOVE AND VIOLENCE **A02**

When Heathcliff's love of Catherine corrupts into a lust for revenge, his passion transgresses powerful social taboos: he lies with her dead body in the grave; he tyrannises his dying son in order to accumulate wealth; and he torments his wife without compunction.

Catherine, unable to reconcile her passion for Heathcliff with her marriage to Edgar, resorts to self-destruction: 'I'll try to break their hearts by breaking my own' (p. 116). She refuses food, wilfully exposes herself to a chill when she is feverish, and works herself up into a nervous agitation while she is carrying Edgar's child. She dies in childbirth, and her daughter is born two months prematurely. The greatest of love stories, then, is explored through the profoundest acts of violence.

NATURE AND CULTURE

The dichotomy between nature and culture, which forms part of the thematic structure of this novel, is played out in the relationship between the two houses: Wuthering Heights, which represents nature, and Thrushcross Grange, representing culture. The theme is developed in the ways in which the houses similarly represent enclosure and exposure. The opposition between these two displays them as both antagonistic and subtly matched. This is a conflict that can be interpreted in a number of ways: in historical terms, as a rural way of life contends against industrialisation; in psychological terms, as a struggle between the ego and the id; in sexual terms, as a choice between experience and representation.

The descriptions of nature in this novel are almost never gratuitous, or simply scene-setting. They have a **symbolic** significance so it is worth paying attention to them. From the very beginning Lockwood identifies himself as a man of culture, appropriately living at the Grange, and utterly incapable of reading the signs of nature. His abortive attempt to negotiate the snowstorm and read the human signs which underlie the elements are testimony to this.

Nature is neither legible nor representable in this novel. Lockwood cannot read its signs, and Catherine refuses to name it. Nor is nature seen as unremittingly cruel in comparison to culture. The representations of culture show it as equally dangerous, and violent, and there are descriptions of the natural world which are tender and refined.

The novel opens with Lockwood's account of the countryside and his impression of his place within it:

> This is certainly a beautiful country! In all England, I do not believe that I could have fixed on a situation so completely removed from the stir of society. A perfect misanthropist's Heaven – and Mr Heathcliff and I are such a suitable pair to divide the desolation between us. (p. 3)

Lockwood inhabits the landscape of the moors as a tourist. As a tourist, he is a consumer, converting the landscape and the lives of its occupants into a private aesthetic experience. He contributes nothing to its maintenance; he fails to understand its dangers or even to read its beauty except in a romanticised and sentimental way. In Nancy Armstrong's essay 'Imperialist Nostalgia and *Wuthering Heights*' (in Linda H. Peterson (ed.), *Wuthering Heights: Case Studies in Contemporary Criticism*, 1992), she argues that 'Lockwood's journey into the wastelands, farms and villages is a journey back in time. As the story regresses through preceding generations of the Earnshaw family, it appears to be taking us back to the primitive beginnings of the culture' (p. 435).

CRITICAL VIEWPOINT A03

Gilbert and Gubar's essay on *Wuthering Heights* sees the opposition of nature and culture in traditionally gendered terms, with culture as male and nature as female. Indeed, they assert that this novel is 'gender-obsessed'. Within the novel, a reading of the gendering of nature as female is supported by the manifestation of the storm as a female witch-child, the original Catherine, in Lockwood's second visionary dream. Heaven and hell are seen in similarly gendered terms. Catherine's choice of culture over nature, in marrying Edgar, is overlaid by her assertion that she has 'no more business to marry Edgar Linton than I have to be in Heaven' (p. 81).

KEY QUOTATION: NATURE AND CULTURE A01

Key quotation:

'"Nelly, *you* have helped to unsettle me! ... Oh, I'm burning! I wish I were out of doors – I wish I were a girl again, half savage and hardy, and free ... and laughing at injuries, not maddening under them! Why am I so changed?"' (p. 125)

Possible interpretations:

- Links can be drawn here to the wider themes of nature versus culture, savagery versus civilisation.
- It refers to the fusion between self and landscape that characterises Catherine and Heathcliff. The reference to childhood also suggests that their relationship is essentially 'innocent'.

STUDY FOCUS: NATURE AND NOSTALGIA · A04

In *Wuthering Heights*, Brontë employs landscape imagery in particular to represent heightened emotional states that would otherwise defy representation in the nineteenth-century novel. Even though the emotions were couched in more or less poetic language, this novel caused such a public outcry upon publication that Charlotte Brontë was required to defend it. Her defence consisted of situating her sister precisely in the nostalgic rural environment that cannot be held responsible for its actions.

To identify the author with the region that she represented, Charlotte infused her with nostalgia. She reframed the novel as something 'rustic all through. It is moorish and wild, and knotty as the root of heath.' Charlotte's preface arrogated these same qualities to the author: 'nor was it natural that it should be otherwise, the author being herself a native and nursling of the moors' (p. li).

CHECK THE BOOK A04

Writing Worlds: Discourse, Text and Metaphor in the Representation of Landscape, edited by Trevor J. Barnes and James. S. Duncan (1992), offers a range of insightful essays focusing on the representations of landscape within a variety of texts.

THE REPRESENTATION OF NATURE

This relationship between landscape and the emotions can be read in both directions. Margaret Homans, in her essay 'Repression and Sublimation of Nature in *Wuthering Heights*' (in Juliann E. Fleenor (ed.), *The Female Gothic*, 1978) takes up a point first made by Leo Bersani about the destructiveness of nature. Pointing out that nature is hardly ever directly represented in this novel which appears to be about nature, Homans argues that Emily Brontë chooses indirect methods such as **metaphor** or **anecdote** as a mode of repressing its more threatening aspects.

PROPERTY AND AMBITION

While we could argue that *Wuthering Heights* is first and foremost a tale of passionate relationships expressed through and reflected in the wild, natural landscape, more worldly aspects also play their part. As Heathcliff turns his anger into a desire for revenge, his ambition for power and property also becomes a driving force in the novel.

STUDY FOCUS: PROPERTY AND INHERITANCE · A01

Heathcliff is able to obtain control of both properties through his clever manipulation of the complex laws of inheritance. When Mr Earnshaw dies there is no mention of a will. Catherine and Hindley therefore inherit all the personal property equally and Wuthering Heights passes to Hindley. Catherine's personal property passes to Edgar upon marriage. Hindley gambles his inheritance away, and on his death it emerges that Heathcliff is the mortgagee of the Heights, so the property is his. The Linton property is different. It has parkland, and is much more of an estate property. In his will, Mr Linton leaves the property to Edgar, his only son. Edgar's daughters are passed over in favour of Mr Linton's daughter Isabella, and her and Heathcliff's son. Heathcliff has no legal right to the property, but he claims the right on behalf of his son and his wife. Heathcliff thus comes into possession of both properties.

MORALITY AND EDUCATION

MORALITY

There are at least three views of morality which are pitted against each other in this novel. Conventional, institutionalised morality might be said to be most forcibly represented by Joseph, and it is shown as pious, restrictive, domineering and legislative. Ever ready with a biblical quotation or religious homily, Joseph provides a relentlessly sour commentary upon the activities of the other members of the Heights household. His is the restrictive voice of social convention which intrudes upon this house of nature, regulating it and judging it.

The second form of morality which is explored in the novel focuses attention upon the morality of authenticity, of being true to the self. In the light of this morality, Catherine's marriage to Edgar is judged as an extreme act of bad faith which precipitates all subsequent tragedy and evil.

The third form of morality which is explored is that of self-interest over altruism. Many of the characters in the novel appear to act for the good of others, and yet their actions serve the aggrandisement of their own power or knowledge. For example, Nelly Dean withholds or reveals her knowledge apparently arbitrarily, but her choices to do so invariably influence the events of the novel. Examples of this are when she neglects to tell Edgar about Catherine's illness and when she informs him of Cathy's correspondence with Linton. On each occasion her decision has profound consequences for the events of the novel.

EDUCATION

Brontë seems ambivalent about the effects of education. The denial of education to Heathcliff is perceived as a form of social punishment and humiliation. It robs Heathcliff of status both within the family and within society. Yet Hareton's painful acquisition of a formal education in the final part of the novel can be read as having both beneficial and negative implications. Hareton acquires the learning and social skills required for union with Cathy; but he also appears to lose power – including sexual power – in his submission to this option. This might be read in terms of a repetition of Catherine's choice earlier in the text, where she trades authentic selfhood for social privilege.

> **CONTEXT** **A04**
>
> Emily and her sisters were relatively well-educated women, since their father permitted them access to all the books in his library, and they were also able to make use of the Mechanics' Institute Library in Keighley.

STUDY FOCUS: EDUCATION VERSUS INTELLIGENCE **A02**

Lockwood prides himself on his educational standing, but repeatedly misreads both his environment and his companions. Education in the form of reading, however, dignifies Nelly Dean in her role as narrator and lends her social status. Brontë appears to make a distinction between education and intelligence, and prizes intelligence, both in terms of information and in terms of emotional wisdom, far above education.

STRUCTURE

DUAL NARRATION

Brontë frames her narrative in terms of a dual narration, a technique that was virtually unprecedented when she wrote *Wuthering Heights*. *Wuthering Heights* has a distinct and complex narrative structure, in that it is a story within a story within a story. One character tells the story to another character, who then tells the story to us. We read a story, told by a woman (Brontë) related by a man (Lockwood) who has been told the story by a woman (Nelly Dean).

Brontë's first **narrator**, Lockwood, who tells the **frame narrative**, is demonstrably unreliable: he mistakes social relationships and radically misreads Heathcliff from the beginning. Although Nelly Dean's narrative is somewhat less subject to contradiction and denial, it is nevertheless evidently informed by her own preferences, and from time to time her ulterior motives. We are never under the illusion that Nelly Dean's is a neutral or objective narrative. The novel explicitly resists such consolations and insists upon the responsibilities of all readers and storytellers, as, for example, when Nelly admits that she 'was deceived, completely, as you will hear' (p. 40) in her assumption that Heathcliff was not vindictive.

CONTEXT — A04

The fairy-tale structure, found in tales like 'Beauty and the Beast', 'Bluebeard' and 'Rumpelstiltskin' permitted women writers to elaborate ideas about choice and love and popular romance within the historical and social context of the marriage contract in the nineteenth century.

CONTEXT — A03

During the 1950s a series of articles appeared in the journal *Nineteenth Century Fiction* which debated the exact role of the narrators. John K. Mathison ('Nelly Dean and the Power of *Wuthering Heights*', 1956) argued that 'Nelly is an admirable woman whose point of view ... the reader must reject', thus forcing the reader 'into an active participation in the book' (p. 106).

Some **feminist** analyses have focused on the fact that Nelly Dean's narrative takes precedence over that of Lockwood, and have seen this as Brontë making an intervention into the male bias of much Victorian literature. Others have read it as a destabilising of the conventional authority of the narrative voice. However we choose to read it, it is clear that there is a redistribution of power when Nelly takes up the narrative. For more on this topic, see **Form: The narrators**.

STUDY FOCUS: NARRATORS OR ACTORS? — A03

In his essay 'The Narrators of *Wuthering Heights*', published in 1957, Carl Woodring argues that Nelly and Lockwood can be read as both narrators and actors in the plot. According to his reading, the narrators are not merely neutral commentators on the action, but active participants in it. This shift of emphasis is a significant one since it focuses not merely on form, but also on character and agency. Having such a complex narrative frame raises many questions which are at the heart of how we read literature, and what our expectations about truth and story might be.

FORM

GENRE

Plot summaries are never sufficiently revealing of the text's effects, which is why the manner of telling the story is as important as the story itself, and also why it is worth paying the same level of attention to form as to content: *how* something is said, as well as just *what* is said.

'A RUDE AND STRANGE PRODUCTION'

Wuthering Heights been noted for its generic ambiguity. Exactly what kind of novel is this 'rude and strange production'? If indeed it is a novel. It has been called an 'expanded fairytale' by Elliot Gose (1972, p. 233), a 'Romantic incest-story: Heathcliff as brother-lover' by Q. D. Leavis (in Rick Rylance (ed.), *Debating Texts*, 1987, p. 145; see also pp. 24–30) and a 'psychological study' by numerous critics both contemporary with the novel and writing today. As Robert Kiely (*The Romantic Novel in England*, 1972) remarks:

> *Wuthering Heights* is like dream *and* like life *and* like history *and* like other works of literature precisely because Brontë rejects the exclusiveness of these categories. They continually inform and define one another. (p. 236)

And it is perhaps precisely this generic uncertainty that continues to fascinate and intrigue so many readers. We can see how the pleasure of the familiar, provided by the text's realism, is challenged by the subversive power of the genres of fantasy and horror. This means that when we read *Wuthering Heights* the enjoyment of the novel's romantic escapism is counterpointed by the stand it takes against convention. *Wuthering Heights* is a novel which causes us to reassess our conventional wisdom, to (re)consider the prejudices that we take for granted, to take delight in contradiction and paradox.

GENRE-BUSTING

Wuthering Heights then has famously been considered a generically puzzling book to categorise, something of a genre-buster, combining elements of many different kinds of genres. With its confident originality it appears to belong to the tradition of the *roman personnel* (the lived fiction). The relationship between art and life provides the central quest for biographer-critics. For example, Brontë's first biographer-critic, A. Mary F. Robinson (*Emily Brontë*, 1883, p. 217), painstakingly traced aspects of Heathcliff's behaviour to aspects of Branwell Brontë, Emily's brother. Biographer-critics saw the task of literary criticism as that of exploring the relationships between fiction and reality. In fact, even Charlotte Brontë's responses to some of the early criticisms of *Wuthering Heights* seem to endorse this kind of critical approach.

Other attempts to categorise the novel have seen it as a **Gothic** novel preoccupied with the fantastic and supernatural; a fairy tale 'in which there is no semblance of reason'; a negotiation of the nineteenth-century **novel of manners**, looking at the relationships between culture and nature; a **Romantic** novel, given its pervading fascination with dreams and the unconscious, and the status it accords the imagination; and a visionary novel, preoccupied with metaphysical issues of mystical politics – witness the contrast Emily Brontë draws between conventional religion and the overarching metaphysical truths of love and unconventional perception.

This focus on genres is not without its implications for our reading of the text, or its characters. Our decisions about what sort of novel this is will influence what we expect to see in the characters, plot and setting.

CONTEXT **A04**

Biographer-critics of the nineteenth century considered the novel as if the key to understanding it lay in drawing parallels between Emily Brontë's life and those of her characters.

CHECK THE BOOK **A04**

Nancy Armstrong (in Stoneman (ed.), *Wuthering Heights: Contemporary Critical Essays*, 1993) argues that the 'enigmatic' figure of Heathcliff is the result of his crossing between literary genres – the Romantic genres of the early nineteenth century, and early Victorian domestic realism.

THE GOTHIC

The **Gothic** is a form marked by ghosts and the supernatural. Ghost stories and horror stories have no doubt always been told, but the Gothic, as a literary tradition, is actually relatively modern. Characteristic of this kind of fiction is the stranglehold of the past upon the present. In Gothic fiction emphasis is placed upon setting: often gloomy castles and windswept, bleak landscapes. Images of ruin and decay are also typical.

By the nineteenth century, the Gothic was a popular form, and examples include Mary Shelley's *Frankenstein*, Charlotte Brontë's *Villette*, Jane Austen's *Northanger Abbey* and Wilkie Collins's *The Woman in White*.

As a form, Gothic literature lends itself to psychological realism, combining atmospheric power and the imaginative range of romance. It is an emotionally charged kind of literature, dealing with the uncanny and the ambiguous.

Gothic narratives are complex and multi-layered. They are given to excess. Ambivalence and contradiction prevent single meanings from being clearly stated. The Gothic is an aesthetic based on feeling and emotion. It is associated with notions of the **sublime.**

CONTEXT A04

The first important instance of the Gothic genre is Horace Walpole's *The Castle of Otranto* (1764).

CHECK THE BOOK A04

Fred Botting's *Critical Introduction to the Gothic* gives a comprehensive account of the history and characterstics of the form. See also *York Notes Companions: Gothic Literature* (2011) by Sue Chaplin.

STUDY FOCUS: *WUTHERING HEIGHTS* AND THE GOTHIC A02

Typical features of the Victorian Gothic include gloomy settings such as prisons or ancient houses. Wuthering Heights is described by Lockwood as decorated with 'a quantity of grotesque carving lavished over the front, and especially about the principal door ... a wilderness of crumbling griffins' (p. 4). Later in the novel, the house serves as a prison for Cathy and Nelly Dean. Also popular in the Gothic imagination are ghosts, monsters and sexual fantasy. Catherine's ghost appears to Lockwood, who describes the room he is given to sleep in as 'swarming with ghosts and goblins!' (p. 27). The powerful attraction between Catherine and Heathcliff extends beyond the grave, and sees Heathcliff digging up Catherine's grave to lie with her (p. 289).

THE NARRATORS

There are two principal **narrators** in this novel, and this is an important device, which throws into question the authority of the narrator. The aim of the classical narrator, as Frederic Jameson has noted in *The Political Unconscious* (1981), is to restore to the experience of reading some of the pleasure of oral storytelling, which has been to a certain extent lost through the medium of printed books.

That is to say, the conventional narrator confers upon the novel something of the authenticity of a spoken narrative. A narrator makes the story seem 'true' in some sense, just as though we were really in the presence of a person recounting the story to us.

STUDY FOCUS: NELLY DEAN – A REVOLUTIONARY SURVIVOR? — A02

The presence of the narrator is comforting, since the narrator is, by virtue of his or her role, a survivor: the narrator must survive to tell the retrospective tale. The narrator has an authority, which is made even more dramatic in nineteenth-century fiction on account of the fact that nearly all narrators are male. It is doubly significant, therefore, that Emily Brontë chooses two narrators, one male and one female, and that the narrative of Nelly Dean outranks and dispossesses that of Lockwood, the male narrator. **Feminist** critiques of the novel have focused on this fact and how unusual and revolutionary it must have seemed to Brontë's Victorian readership.

READING BETWEEN THE LINES

The construction of two narrators, neither of which is seen to be entirely reliable or impartial, provides for the reader a means of reading what the **post-structuralist** critic Pierre Macherey has called the 'not-said'. By reading 'between the lines' of Nelly's and Lockwood's narratives, the reader is able to interpret information from the text which is never made explicit. In distinguishing between 'reliable' and 'unreliable' accounts, therefore, the reader is able to construct a body of knowledge from which to make judgements about the text, and its characters. As Catherine Belsey points out in *Critical Practice* (1980):

> In *Wuthering Heights* the inadequacies of the perceptions of Lockwood or Nellie [*sic*] Dean do not prevent the reader from seeming to apprehend the real nature of the relationship between Catherine and Heathcliff. (p. 78)

The fact that we can perceive the accounts given by the narrators as biased and informed by ideology permits us to read what the narrators literally *cannot* tell us. A good example of this is in Volume I, Chapter II, when Lockwood mistakes the family relationships at Wuthering Heights:

> 'It is strange … how custom can mould our tastes and ideas; many could not imagine the existence of happiness in a life of such complete exile from the world as you spend, Mr Heathcliff; yet, I'll venture to say, that, surrounded by your family, and with your amiable lady as the presiding genius over your home and heart –' (p. 13)

Lockwood cannot tell us that his ideological assumptions forbid him to perceive the complex relationship between Heathcliff and Cathy, and yet he is able to alert us to that fact.

LANGUAGE

DIALECT

Emily Brontë's use of the Yorkshire dialect has generally been considered to be an accurate account of the accent of the region. In the second edition of the novel, which was edited and amended by Charlotte Brontë, Charlotte changed the way in which Emily had written Joseph's dialect in order to make it more comprehensible. Over time, Charlotte's edition has fallen from favour and most modern editions now take the first edition as their starting point. However, this use of dialect possibly earned *Wuthering Heights* some of its early hostile reviews, since the language and manners of the local characters were criticised for being rough and coarse.

CHECK THE BOOK — A04

Psychoanalytic theorists such as Jay Clayton (1987) have drawn on the Lacanian view of language as alienating, and alienation as a crucial part of what it means to be human, to consider Brontë's use of dialect and language style in her novel.

Writing dialect as it sounds is a sensitive issue, since it can make for uncomfortable reading and so make it hard to warm to or understand that character. However, if we take Joseph as an example, his dialect does not serve to make him ridiculous, but rather contributes to our interpretation of his authentic character. We read Joseph as cantankerous, moralising, unyielding and inflexible. His dialect is evidence of his resistance to change and his hostility to strangers. It literally makes him 'difficult to read' or to understand. It thus underlines something in his character. It also emphasises to us that Joseph is proudly himself, unwilling to make that self more palatable to people whose values and world view might differ widely from his own.

Nelly Dean would undoubtedly understand and use this dialect herself, but Brontë's decision to write her speech in standard English serves to emphasise the fact that she is flexible and capable of using and understanding different **discourses** according to her audience. It also suggests that Nelly can manipulate information according to her interests. Thus we can see Brontë's deliberate choice of writing, now in dialect and now in 'heard English', as an expression of character and identity.

POETIC LANGUAGE

The superabundance of **metaphor** and **symbol** and the lyricism of the descriptive passages have earned this novel praise for its poetic language:

One time, however, we were near quarrelling. He said the pleasantest manner of spending a hot July day was lying from morning till evening on a bank of heath in the middle of the moors, with the bees humming dreamily about among the bloom, and the larks singing high up over head, and the blue sky, and bright sun shining steadily and cloudlessly. That was his most perfect idea of heaven's happiness – mine was rocking in a rustling green tree, with a west wind blowing, and bright, white clouds flitting rapidly above; and not only larks, but throstles, and blackbirds, and linnets, and cuckoos pouring out music on every side, and the moors seen at a distance, broken into cool, dusky dells; but close by great swells of long grass undulating in waves to the breeze; and the woods and sounding water, and the whole world awake and wild with joy. He wanted all to lie in an ecstasy of peace; I wanted all to sparkle, and dance in a glorious jubilee. (p. 248)

Brontë's evident delight in the sensual life and the pleasure she takes in language are given full latitude in such passages. Lord David Cecil (1958) praises the rhythm of Brontë's prose as 'unfailingly beautiful; a varied, natural, haunting cadence, now buoyantly lilting, now surging like the sea' (p. 191). In fact, in this novel there are numerous correspondences with Emily Brontë's poetry.

IMAGERY AND SYMBOLISM

ANIMAL IMAGERY

Brontë frequently uses animal imagery as a metaphor for some human frailty or moral deficiency: Linton, for example, is described as a 'chicken' p. 207), Hareton a 'dog' (p. 310), Heathcliff a 'mad dog' (p. 162) and a 'savage beast' (p. 169). Lockwood's mistaken apprehension of a heap of dead rabbits as a chairful of cats identifies him not only as unobservant, but also as someone who is incapable of reading animal imagery. Given the preponderance of such imagery in this novel, it is therefore entirely appropriate that his narratorial role is quickly taken over by Nelly Dean. The description of the male characters in this novel as beasts can be read as underscoring Catherine as a reluctant bride.

As Mark Schorer ('Fiction and the Matrix of Analogy', *Kenyon Review* 11:4, 1949) points out, most of the metaphorical references to animals in *Wuthering Heights* are references to wild animals: 'Hareton's whiskers encroached *bearishly* over his cheeks', and Heathcliff denies the paternity of 'that bear'; Heathcliff is a 'fierce, pitiless, *wolfish* man' (p. 547).

For the *Christian Remembrancer* in 1857, the recognition that Emily Brontë's 'heroine's scratch and tear, and bite, and slap … The men … roll, and grapple, and struggle, and throttle and clutch and tear and trample' was clear evidence of her moral degradation.

Clifton Snider has given a comprehensive account of the animal imagery in this novel, reading such imagery in terms of vampiric **archetypes.** He points out that this is a novel rife with vicious animals: that it is the bite from the Thrushcross Grange guard dog, Skulker, which presents the initial disruption in the childhood relationship between Catherine and Heathcliff, and that Heathcliff himself is described as both supernatural – a 'demon' – and animal – a 'mad dog'.

DREAMS AND THE SUPERNATURAL

Dreams are an important key to knowledge in this novel, and the dreams and hallucinatory elements of the text have anticipated twentieth-century **psychoanalytic criticism.**

Dreams demonstrate a way of thinking through the forbidden. They are equipped with a magic all their own. In the novel, dreams are clearly of central importance and their relation to magic, visions and ghostly apparitions is never understated.

Lockwood's dream of the child Cathy begging to be let in is disturbing on two levels. It is grisly, and the gratuitous cruelty of him sawing her wrist against the broken glass is uncomfortable. But as Frank Kermode (*The Classic*, 1975) suggests, it is also disturbing because neither Lockwood nor Heathcliff really believes that it was a dream. It therefore doubly resists any attempts to think about it in rational terms.

The extravagance of the ghostly, the supernatural and the unearthly in this novel is entirely devoted to the relationship between Catherine and Heathcliff, and to descriptions of them as individuals. This achieves its most profound exemplification when Catherine is dying, and Heathcliff is described by Nelly as a 'creature [not] of my own species' (p. 162), and then again towards the end of the novel when she wonders 'Is he a ghoul, or a vampire?' (p. 330). As Clifton Snider suggests, Brontë's decision to make Heathcliff her hero can be read as an intervention into the Victorian prejudice against outsiders, such as gypsies and beggars, as well as their fascination for and prejudice against the supernatural.

Frank Kermode (1975) considers the dreams of the novel in his analysis, paying particular attention to the 'vision' that Nelly has by the signpost of the child Hindley who 'turns into' Hareton, who in turn 'turns into' Heathcliff. He argues that although not strictly a dream this has many similarities with a real dream in terms of its transformations and displacements. The confusion of generations, Hindley, Hareton and Heathcliff mingling and merging, qualifies our sense of their identities and the sense of all narrative explanations offered in the text. Because Brontë refuses to offer us any naturalistic explanation of Nelly's

CONTEXT A04

In her childhood, Emily Brontë was influenced by the household servants who recounted supernatural tales set in northern England.

experience, it joins the other instances of occult phenomena which are 'only indeterminately related to the natural narrative. And this serves to muddle routine single readings, to confound explanation and expectation, and to make necessary a full recognition of the intrinsic **plurality** of the text' (p. 129).

LANDSCAPE IMAGERY

Many critics have paid attention to Brontë's use of landscape imagery, and the way in which landscape frequently functions as a **metaphor** for human behaviour or characteristics in this novel. Mark Schorer (1949) notes that 'Human conditions are like the activities of the landscape, where rains flood … spirits are at high water mark … illnesses are weathered' (p. 545).

Faces, too, are like landscapes, with countenances regularly clouding over and then brightening. Catherine experiences whole 'seasons of gloom', and 'her humour was a mere vane for constantly varying caprices' (p. 160).

It is worth considering what the implications of this are for your understanding both of the characters and of the landscape, because the associations work both ways. We first see the landscape through Lockwood's eyes as difficult to navigate, and hostile, and the first characters he encounters also exhibit these qualities. By the end of the novel, when all the conflicts are resolved, his closing remarks detail the 'benign sky', and the 'quiet earth' (p. 337).

Although by now we know not to trust Lockwood's account entirely, we can nevertheless assume that these two conflicting descriptions of the landscape serve not as pure setting, but as a commentary on the nature and lives of the inhabitants of that landscape.

HISTORICAL BACKGROUND

SOCIAL AND ECONOMIC CONTEXT

Emily Brontë's contemporary readers would have been unsurprised by the story of Heathcliff as a foundling from the port of Liverpool: orphans, foundlings and child beggars were a common social problem in the nineteenth century. When families were unable to feed or protect their children, they left them in workhouses and churches in the hope that Christian charity or social justice would look after them. Indeed, Heathcliff's background, tantalisingly obscure as it might seem within the novel, can be read against the social upheavals of Brontë's own time, the key factor in which was the Industrial Revolution.

The effects of the first Industrial Revolution in the late eighteenth century, when the novel is set, were profoundly felt in almost every aspect of daily life. These effects became increasingly tangible through the nineteenth century and would have been well known to early readers of the novel. The mechanisation of industries such as the textile industry meant increased productivity and trade expansion. This in turn saw an enormous shift in the population from rural communities dependent on agriculture, to the towns and cities which swelled in population. The romantic and nostalgic references to nature and the moors as a place of childhood paradise in *Wuthering Heights* might also be read in this context.

PROPERTY LAWS IN THE EIGHTEENTH CENTURY

Key to understanding the plot of *Wuthering Heights* is an appreciation of how the inheritance laws worked in favour of men and against women's interests in the eighteenth century. According to these laws, Catherine Linton cannot inherit Thrushcross Grange when her father dies. Instead, the property automatically passes to Linton Heathcliff as Isabella's son, because males have precedence over females in the inheritance of property. However, should Linton die the property would revert to Catherine Linton, as the sole surviving heir. It is for this reason that Heathcliff is so keen for Catherine and Linton to marry, for once they are married and Catherine is his daughter-in-law, her property automatically becomes his.

MEN AND WOMEN

Inequality between men and women in society extended into every area. It is therefore possible to read *Wuthering Heights* as an extraordinary critique of the social conditions for women, since, as Eva Figes points out in *Sex and Subterfuge: Women Writers in 1850* (1982), Victorian women writers had been largely prevented from writing social or political criticism in their novels owing to their vulnerable position as women writing in a male-dominated cultural milieu. The rural setting of *Wuthering Heights* can be seen as indicative of the position of women as isolated from culture and modern industry, though it also accurately reflects Emily Brontë's own lived experience. The emphasis upon the struggle between nature and culture, north and south, folklore and science, can be recognised as being particularly disturbing to its contemporary readership.

CONTEXT **A04**

The Irish potato famine (1845–52), caused by a potato blight, brought thousands of refugees to the port of Liverpool. During the famine more than a million people died in Ireland and another million emigrated. The impact of the blight upon a population almost entirely dependent on the potato for food was extensive.

REVOLUTION

The historical period that is covered in the course of the novel's events was a time of enormous social upheaval, seeing both the American Revolution, in which thirteen colonies broke away from the British Empire to become the United States of America and rejected the authority of the British Government to govern their territories, and the French Revolution, which had an enormous impact upon the whole of Europe. It is possible to read Heathcliff as a revolutionary figure, a man not born into social rank but nevertheless contriving to bring down the old establishment of two powerful houses.

LITERARY BACKGROUND

Emphasis upon a literary context for the novel has been threefold. First, critics have pointed out the poetic qualities of the novel and have cited the influence of Byron (see portrait, right). Indeed, a common critical reading of Heathcliff is to see him as a **Byronic hero**, following a review in *The Examiner* in 1848. More sophisticated modern versions of this approach include Gilbert and Gubar's reading in *The Madwoman in the Attic*, where they consider the novel as a revision of the Miltonic myth of the Fall, and Harold Bloom's reading of the novel as a critique of Byron's *Manfred*. Such readings see literature as part of the real life we lead, not just reflective of it, and argue that the literary texts we create respond to and modify those we have read. The Byronic influences have been particularly discussed by Winifred Gerin in her biography of Emily Brontë.

A second source of influence has been considered to be the **Gothic** romance, and critics have read the significance of ghosts and dreams in this context. *Wuthering Heights* is rich in all the elements typical to the form of the Gothic romance. Parallels might be drawn with Mary Shelley's *Frankenstein*, for example, with the theme of the divided and monstrous self being played out in the character of Heathcliff. For more on the Gothic, see **Part Four: Form**.

A third strand of literary influence might be seen to be the effect of fictional realism. According to the Victorian critic Matthew Arnold, realist fiction amounts to a 'criticism of life'. In realist fiction, plots have the fluidity of life and the characters are endowed with psychological, social or natural authenticity. Realist fiction, then, leads people to draw conclusions not just about books but about life in general, and so literature has a moral obligation to be true.

CRITICAL VIEWPOINT **A03**

The Gothic romance was a popular form of writing in the eighteenth and nineteenth centuries. It generally dealt with the supernatural and the fantastical. Heathcliff's desire for Catherine, which extends beyond the grave, can be seen in this context. Gilbert and Gubar (*The Madwoman in the Attic: The Woman Writer and the Nineteenth-Century Literary Imagination*, 1979) famously suggest the possibility of *Wuthering Heights* as a 'deliberate copy' of Mary Shelley's *Frankenstein*.

FAMILY INFLUENCES

Following the deaths of their mother and two elder sisters in the 1820s, Charlotte, Emily, Anne and Branwell Brontë were brought up by their aunt in the parsonage at Haworth (see photo, left) and lived relatively remotely from their community, as Charlotte explains in the biographical notice which prefaces most editions of the text of *Wuthering Heights*. They took their chief enjoyment from literary compositions which they invented for each other, most famously the sagas of the mythical islands of Gondal which inspired their later poetry. The poetic quality of Emily Brontë's writing in *Wuthering Heights* has been seen as one of the novel's greatest strengths.

CRITICAL DEBATES

RECEPTION AND EARLY REVIEWS

A number of early reviews of the novel praised it for its imaginative potency while criticising it for being strange and ambiguous. In a biographical notice attached to many modern versions of the novel, Charlotte Brontë (see portrait, right) complains that the novel did not receive sufficient merit at its initial reception. But *Wuthering Heights* did not go unrecognised by its early readers. Literary critics repeatedly acknowledged its originality, genius and imaginative power – even if they also complained about its moral ambiguity.

Following Charlotte Brontë's clarification of the gender of Ellis Bell, Victorian readers began to place *Wuthering Heights* in the Gothic category, a category of literature peculiarly associated with women. Dante Gabriel Rossetti, in 1854, describes *Wuthering Heights* as 'a fiend of a book, an incredible monster, combining all the stronger female tendencies from Mrs Browning to Mrs Brownrigg. The action is laid in Hell, – only it seems places and people have no English names there.'

For the Victorians, *Wuthering Heights* was unarguably an immoral and uncivilised book. It deeply challenged all their ideas about propriety and literature. Equally, by the 1920s it was just as clear that its great value and message was metaphysical. Lord David Cecil, Professor of English Literature at Oxford, helped to integrate *Wuthering Heights* into the canon of English Literature in his famous chapter in *Early Victorian Novelists* (1934). He argues that Brontë's motivation in *Wuthering Heights* was an exploration of the meaning of life: 'Her great characters exist in virtue of the reality of their attitude to the universe; they look before us on the simple epic outline which is all that we see of man when revealed against the huge landscape of the cosmic scene' (p. 151).

NINETEENTH-CENTURY VIEWS

Following Charlotte's lead, some nineteenth-century analyses of *Wuthering Heights* emphasised the psychological elements of the novel's plot and characters. The critic Sydney Dobell praised Emily Brontë for her portrayal of the 'deep unconscious' truth of Catherine Earnshaw's personality (in E. Jolly (ed.), *The Life and Letters of Sydney Dobell*, vol. 1, 1878, pp. 169–74). However, Dobell insisted that *Wuthering Heights* was not by Emily but was an early work by Charlotte Brontë. According to Dobell, Charlotte Brontë understood that 'certain crimes and sorrows are not so much the result of intrinsic evil as of a false position in the scheme of things'. Dobell's is a view that anticipates some **feminist** discussions of Catherine's decisions and the consequences of those decisions.

Much early criticism tended to look to Emily Brontë's life to understand elements in her work. Such criticism is based on a view that the relationship between literature and the world is relatively straightforward, that reality exists, and that it is literature's job to describe it. The role of literary criticism, according to this view, is to assess the accuracy of the representations, and also to assess the moral content of the work, for literature and the arts in general were held to be an integral part of the civilised life, and thus should contribute to the moral fabric of society.

TWENTIETH-CENTURY VIEWS

Close critical attention to Brontë's novel begins with C. P. Sanger (*The Structure of Wuthering Heights*, 1926) and Lord David Cecil (*Early Victorian Novelists*, 1935), both of whom wished to distance criticism from moral judgement and to proceed from an analysis of the formal elements of the text. Cecil's elaboration of the 'storm and calm' structure of *Wuthering Heights* has become one of the most widely accepted of all readings. He argues that the novel is based on a foundation of the dynamic relation between two spiritual principles:

CHECK THE BOOK **A04**

Patsy Stoneman (*Wuthering Heights: Contemporary Critical Essays*, 1993) offers an accessible and representative selection of early reviews of *Wuthering Heights*.

CHECK THE FILM **A04**

There have been many film versions of the novel, the earliest of which was A. V. Bramble's 1920 silent film.

the principle of storm – of the harsh, the ruthless, the wild, the dynamic; and … the principle of calm – of the gentle, the merciful, the passive and the tame … in spite of their apparent opposition these principles are not conflicting. (Cecil, *Early Victorian Novelists*, revised edition, 1958, p. 151)

Critics such as Cecil and Sanger prepared the ground for the **new critics** such as Mark Schorer. Schorer was the first to investigate patterns of imagery in *Wuthering Heights*, in 1949. He sees the novel as a moral story about the futility of grand passion. Other new critics include Dorothy Van Ghent, who drew attention to the metaphors of windows and thresholds.

CONTEMPORARY APPROACHES

MARXIST RESPONSES

Marxist criticism has seen the novel in terms of its social context, looking for connections between the novel and the political, social and economic conditions under which it was produced.

WILSON

CHECK THE BOOK A04

Wilson's purpose in such a reading is to account for the real social conditions in which a book like *Wuthering Heights* was produced, seeing it neither as the product of isolated genius nor as the muddled ramblings of a social recluse. For a confirmation of the effect of the Industrial Revolution on Haworth, see Juliet Barker's biography of the Brontës (1994).

The first consistent attempt to read *Wuthering Heights* in terms of class oppression and struggle was David Wilson's article 'Emily Brontë: First of the Moderns' (1947). Distancing himself from the biographical theories of the novel's origins, Wilson dedicates his reading to the project of picturing 'Emily Brontë in a new light, the light of West Riding social history' (p. 94). He provides a detailed history of Haworth (pictured, right) and its region, describing the freedom of its independent yeomen in medieval times, both from the feudal system and from the Roman Church, suggesting that Haworth was a proudly politicised place from its early days. He continues by describing how mechanised industry devastated local hand-loom weavers and gives detailed evidence that 'these social storms were far too near for the sisters to have lived the quiet secluded lives that have been pictured' (p. 96).

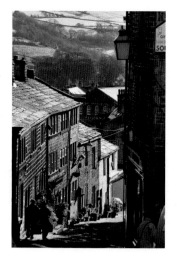

EAGLETON

Perhaps the most famous Marxist analysis of the novel is given by Terry Eagleton in *Myths of Power: A Marxist Study of the Brontës* (1975), in which he considers the novel in terms of its reference to class, economics and history. Eagleton is interested in the novel's relationship to Victorian **ideology**, looking at how that ideology is both reflected and produced by the novel.

Wuthering Heights is ideological, argues Eagleton, because it presents a 'world-view' – it represents conflicts without being fragmented by conflict itself. Contradictions and oppositions coexist in this novel in a profound but not unsatisfying tension.

CRITICAL VIEWPOINT A03

Eagleton argues that although it is possible to read Heathcliff as participating in an economic structure, he can also, because of his unknown origins, be read as 'a purely atomised individual … outside the family and society in an opposing realm which can be adequately imaged only as "Nature"'.

The primary contradiction that Eagleton explores in relation to this assertion is the choice that Catherine must make between Edgar Linton and Heathcliff. He identifies that choice as the pivotal event of the novel and the precipitating factor in all the tragic events which follow. Catherine chooses Edgar Linton because of his social superiority, which Eagleton identifies as an act of 'bad faith', and she is, he judges, rightly criticised by Heathcliff for this betrayal of their more authentic love. The social self, Eagleton argues, is shown to be false not because it is only apparent – Catherine's love for Edgar is not simulated – but because it exists in a contradictory and negative relationship to authentic selfhood, which is shown in Catherine's love of Heathcliff.

Eagleton's essay also analyses Heathcliff's position in the novel in terms of his place in the family structure, local society and the economic system of rural Yorkshire at the turn of the century. Because Heathcliff is spirited out of nowhere into this family, he has no social or domestic status and he is therefore both a threat to the established order and an opportunity for it to be reinvented. Heathcliff disturbs the establishment because he has no legitimate place in its system. Eagleton's analysis turns on the issue of liberty and oppression. The fact that there is no opportunity for freedom either within or outside the system is a consequence of bourgeois society.

Heathcliff learns to see culture as a means of oppression, and he acquires it to use as a weapon. This association of culture with violence is further played out in the novel in the ferocity which is used to defend property, from the moment that Catherine is savaged by Skulker, the Linton's bulldog, to the complex seizure of property by Heathcliff in the second part of the novel.

STUDY FOCUS: HEATHCLIFF'S CONTRADICTION (A03)

In social terms the Heights can be read as embodying the world of the gentleman farmer – the petty-bourgeois yeoman – whereas the Grange epitomises the gentry. Eagleton argues that Heathcliff's social relation to both the Heights and the Grange is one of the most complex issues in the novel. Heathcliff fiercely highlights the contradictions between the two worlds in opposing the Grange and undermining the Heights. He embodies a passionate human protest against the marriage market values of both the Heights and the Grange, while violently caricaturing precisely those values in his calculatedly callous marriage to Isabella. In this Heathcliff can be seen to be a parody of capitalist activity, yet he is not simply this, for he is also a product of and participant in that system. The contradiction of the novel is that Heathcliff both embodies and antagonises the values that he wishes to contest.

The ending of the novel, with its ostensible integration of the values of the two worlds, might seem to weaken Eagleton's argument that the contradictions of the novel coexist in an exciting and productive tension. However, he argues that this conclusion depends upon how one reads Hareton Earnshaw. If Hareton is read as a surrogate and diluted Heathcliff, then the novel's ending does indeed suggest a reconciliation between the gentry and the capitalist. If, however, Hareton is read as a literal survivor of yeoman stock, then what effectively happens is that he is entirely conquered by the **hegemony** or authority of the Grange.

WILLIAMS

Two years before Eagleton's *Myths of Power*, the Marxist critic Raymond Williams had published an insightful reading of *Wuthering Heights* in his book *The Country and the City* (1973), accounting for the relationship between Catherine and Heathcliff in terms of alienation rather than oppression. Although he acknowledges that it is class and property that divide Heathcliff and Catherine, he argues that the solution to their division is never conceived in terms of social reform. What Brontë privileges above all, he argues, is human intensity and a profound connection between people:

> The tragic separation between human intensity and any available social settlement is accepted from the beginning in the whole design and idiom of the novel. The … plot is … sustained by a single feeling, which is the act of transcendence. (p. 176)

This concept of transcendence as a response to alienation from social possibilities is also important in Eagleton's reading.

FEMINIST RESPONSES

GILBERT AND GUBAR

Feminist criticism has seen the novel in terms of its language, and in terms of the strategies and opportunities that are open to women in the novel. Feminist and gender criticism has also provided some interesting readings of the ambivalent representations of

---

CONTEXT (A04)

Because Marxists see ideology as what makes people choose to cooperate with, endorse and naturalise the class structure, they are particularly interested in the contradictions which arise at boundaries between classes and other social groups. To Marxists these contradictions reveal ideology for what it is: an imposed set of beliefs, and not the 'natural order' of things, or inevitable.

CHECK THE BOOK (A04)

Marxist Literary Theory, edited by Terry Eagleton and Drew Milne (1996), offers a superb collection of Marxist essays, giving a good sense of the historical formation of a Marxist literary tradition.

CRITICAL VIEWPOINT A03

When he is referred to as 'Mr Heathcliff' by Lockwood (p. 13), this is instructive for it reveals that Lockwood's relationship with Heathcliff is as misguided as many of his other assumptions.

gender in *Wuthering Heights*, not least of which is Gilbert and Gubar's reading of Heathcliff as 'female' in the sense that second sons, bastards and daughters are female. Heathcliff is 'female' because he is dispossessed of social power. He has no status, no social place and no property. For the majority of the novel, he is only Heathcliff, never Mr Heathcliff, or the Master, in contrast to Edgar Linton. Heathcliff's rebellions against the social conventions of class, marriage and inheritance similarly suggest that he can be read as 'female' since endorsing such conventions only serves the interests of patriarchal culture.

This reading of Heathcliff as female seems to go against the grain of conventional critical agreement that he epitomises heroic masculinity, especially when compared with the fair, slim, soft Edgar. But when these characters are read in terms of their social power, Heathcliff has no social position, and Edgar is always referred to as 'the Master'. Edgar, who is most at home in the library, has all the power of masculine culture behind him. His mastery is contained in documents, books, rent-rolls, patriarchal domination. Edgar is the guardian of culture. Heathcliff is feminine in the sense that he is unpropertied, dispossessed, subject to the rule of the father, an outcast.

In *The Madwoman in the Attic*, Gilbert and Gubar interrogate *Wuthering Heights* in terms of what they term '**feminist** mythologies'. They see the project of the novel as rewriting and revising the Miltonic myth of the Fall. They also identify the novel as a distinctively nineteenth-century response to the problems of origins, and as an exploration into the nature of heaven and hell.

In their reading of the novel in terms of writing against the male tradition, Gilbert and Gubar see *Wuthering Heights* as a 'Bible of Hell', a novel which values the natural over the cultural, the anarchic over the world of organised repression. Wuthering Heights, the house of the title, is hellish by conventional standards, but for Catherine and Heathcliff it represents the kind of non-hierarchical social space in which they are permitted a degree of power which would be denied them elsewhere, since she is female and he is illegitimate, and they are both thereby excluded from power in the conventional world. Thrushcross Grange, across the moor, home of the Linton family and inspired by Shibden Hall in West Yorkshire (pictured), represents the standards of patriarchal culture which will be triumphant by the end of the story, but which the novel itself, through its sympathies for Catherine and Heathcliff, implicitly attacks.

CONTEXT A04

All feminist critical approaches to literature, whatever other traditions they borrow from, share a commitment to place women at the centre of the literary-critical discourses.

STUDY FOCUS: IDENTITY AND MIRRORING   A03

Focusing on the issue of naming in the novel, Gilbert and Gubar suggest that the writing of the name 'Catherine' in its various manifestations, which Lockwood encounters inscribed into the windowsill, reveals the crucial lack of identity that is common to all women under patriarchy: 'What Catherine, or any girl must learn is that she does not know her own name, and therefore cannot know who she is or whom she is destined to be' (p. 276).

However, as Gilbert and Gubar point out, although Heathcliff can be read as Catherine's other self, he is not her identical double. This was a point first made by Leo Bersani in his book *A Future for Astyanax*. Not only is he male and she female, but he is a survivor, and a usurper of power, while she is a mournful, outcast, ghost. Nevertheless, his fate at the end of the novel mirrors hers: he is unable to eat; he is feverish, and obsessed by the elements; and his death is partly a result of his encounter with culture, in the form of Cathy, who as Edgar Linton's daughter embodies the intervention of patriarchy. And in death, Heathcliff has arranged that his body shall merge with Catherine's until they are indistinguishable.

CONTEXT A04

Jacobs's article reminds us of the importance of the material, social aspect of *Wuthering Heights* as it relates to women.

JACOBS

Other feminist critics also make connections between the form of the novel and the historical position of women. Naomi Jacobs, in 'Gender and Layered Narrative in *Wuthering Heights* and *The Tenant of Wildfell Hall*' (1986), gives a legal-social dimension to the question of the narrative frame, suggesting that the process of exposing the real constraints of women's lives indicates at least a partial loosening of those constraints. The argument is that Emily Brontë's challenging of the formal authoritative discourses of Victorian life itself represents a radical intervention into those structures. She proceeds to document the prevalence of nineteenth-century wife abuse and the reluctance of reviewers to acknowledge its existence. Jacobs then argues that the narrative structure of the novel represents an authorial strategy for dealing with the unacceptability of the subject matter.

DECONSTRUCTIVE RESPONSES

J. Hillis Miller has provided an influential deconstructive reading of the novel. **Deconstruction** offers an alternative to traditional scholarship that is both playful and challenging. Unwilling to privilege a certain kind of reading, deconstructive criticism argues that there is no one right way to read a text, and that literature does not contain the kinds of unified and universal truths that traditional criticism seeks. Instead, deconstructive criticism considers the way in which all **transcendent** truths, including those judgements we might make about the aesthetic unity of the text, and the inherent truth of the narrative, undo themselves in internal contradictions and incompatibilities. Hillis Miller's reading focuses upon the ways in which the novel resists rational explanation, for example through its structure, language and use of narrators.

'Structure' is a complex term which can be used to refer to many different features of a text. The aspect of *Wuthering Heights* which has generated the most persistent debate is what might be termed its 'narrative structure': namely, the allocation of different parts of the story to different voices, rather than the more conventional narrative form in which one narrator tells his or her story.

C. P. Sanger (1926) was among the first critics to argue that the structure of *Wuthering Heights* does in fact conform to a logical strictness and exactitude with regard to its dates. He also argues that the most obvious thing about the structure of the story is the symmetry of the family pedigree: for Sanger, the whole intricate structure 'demonstrates the vividness of the author's imagination' (p. 20).

PSYCHOANALYTIC RESPONSES

Psychoanalytic readings of *Wuthering Heights* have offered some very rich insights into the novel. Several Victorian critics, perhaps most famously Sydney Dobell (1850), saw the exciting possibilites of considering the text as a study in abnormal psychology. Freudian psychoanalytic theory has offered critics a more precise vocabulary and a more robust explanation for the obsessive and divided mentalities we see in Heathcliff and Catherine.

Because of its nature, the unconscious is normally inaccessible to the conscious mind. Therefore we must pay attention to the secret ways in which it might reveal itself. One of these ways is through dreams, and one of Freud's earliest published works was *The Interpretation of Dreams* (1900). With its emphasis upon dreams that disrupt the smooth flowing of the narrative, and which are hard to assimilate into the main body of the text, *Wuthering Heights* has proved rich territory for dream interpretation, with Lockwood's dreams in Volume I, Chapter III, providing clues to both the plot and the emotions of the characters.

Many modern psychoanalytical studies of *Wuthering Heights* derive not from Freud but from the theories of Jacques Lacan, whose ideas have been of particular interest to literary critics because of their focus on language. Philip K. Wion has made great use of Lacan's theories about language and about the relationship between the child and the mother in his readings of *Wuthering Heights* (see **Extended commentary: Volume I, Chapter IX**). Wion presents the absence of mothers as a key feature of *Wuthering Heights*, which, he argues, can be attributed to the fact that Emily Brontë's mother died when she was three years old. Lacan suggests that the loss of the mother is an essential part of the human condition, and it can be argued that this makes the novel deeply relevant to all who read it.

CONTEXT A04

Victorian reviewers criticised the novel for its confusing structure since it contradicted their belief that it was the novelist's duty to make his or her meaning plain. The multitude of conflicting voices in this novel serves to disturb any such notions of clear and stable meanings.

PART SIX: GRADE BOOSTER

ASSESSMENT FOCUS

WHAT ARE YOU BEING ASKED TO FOCUS ON?

The questions or tasks you are set will be based around the four **Assessment Objectives, AO1 to AO4.**

You may get more marks for certain **AOs** than others depending on which unit you're working on. Check with your teacher if you are unsure.

WHAT DO THESE AOS ACTUALLY MEAN?

	ASSESSMENT OBJECTIVES	MEANING?
AO1	Articulate creative, informed and relevant responses to literary texts, using appropriate terminology and concepts, and coherent, accurate written expression.	You write about texts in accurate, clear and precise ways so that what you have to say is clear to the marker. You use literary terms (e.g. **palimpsest**) or refer to concepts (e.g. **discourse**) in relevant places.
AO2	Demonstrate detailed critical understanding in analysing the ways in which structure, form and language shape meanings in literary texts.	You show that you understand the specific techniques and methods used by the writer(s) to create the text (e.g. imagery, foreshadowing). You can explain clearly how these methods affect the meaning.
AO3	Explore connections and comparisons between different literary texts, informed by interpretations of other readers.	You are able to see relevant links between different texts. You are able to comment on how others (such as critics) view the text.
AO4	Demonstrate understanding of the significance and influence of the contexts in which literary texts are written and received.	You can explain how social, historical, political or personal backgrounds to the texts affected the writer and how the texts were read when they were first published and at different times since.

WHAT DOES THIS MEAN FOR YOUR STUDY OR REVISION OF *WUTHERING HEIGHTS*?

Depending on the course you are following, you could be asked to:

- Respond to a general question that asks about the text as a whole. For example:

Explore how Brontë presents extremes of behaviour in the novel.

- Write about an aspect of *Wuthering Heights* which is also a feature of other texts you are studying. These questions may take the form of a challenging statement or quotation which you are invited to discuss. For example:

'In *Wuthering Heights* death is seen as a welcome release from the tortures of living.' How far do you agree with this view of the novel?

- Focus on the particular similarities, links, contrasts and differences between this text and others. For example:

Compare and contrast the ways in which the breakdown of normal moral and social codes is explored by Emily Brontë in *Wuthering Heights* and in the other text(s) you are studying.

TARGETING A HIGH GRADE

It is very important to understand the progression from a lower grade to a high grade. In all cases, it is not enough simply to mention some key points and references – instead, you should explore them in depth, drawing out what is interesting and relevant to the question or issue.

TYPICAL C GRADE FEATURES

	FEATURES	EXAMPLES
AO1	You use critical vocabulary accurately, and your arguments make sense, are relevant and focus on the task. You show detailed knowledge of the text.	*Nelly Dean is both a character and a narrator in "Wuthering Heights". Her view of the situation is largely the main perspective in the novel.*
AO2	You can say how some specific aspects of form, structure and language shape meanings.	*"Wuthering Heights" has both a repetitive and complex structure that is based around two houses: Thrushcross Grange and Wuthering Heights. The story is also told by two narrators, who move between the two houses, which may be seen to represent opposites.*
AO3	You consider in detail the connections between texts and also how interpretations of texts differ, with some relevant supporting references.	*Some critics have seen Heathcliff as an example of a Byronic hero, because he is unconventional and rises to a very powerful position from his roots as an orphan. Captain Wentworth in Jane Austen's novel "Persuasion" is similarly a man who has risen in fortunes from humble beginnings.*
AO4	You can write about a range of contextual factors and make some specific and detailed links between these and the task or text.	*Emily Brontë's early personal experience of death had a profound influence upon her writing of this novel, in which each child has at least one parent who dies.*

TYPICAL FEATURES OF AN A OR A* RESPONSE

	FEATURES	EXAMPLES
AO1	You use appropriate critical vocabulary and a technically fluent style. Your arguments are well structured, coherent and always relevant, with a very sharp focus on task.	*The dual narration in "Wuthering Heights" means that multiple perspectives compete with and contradict each other, so that the reader's understanding of character and plot development is constantly revised.*
AO2	You explore and analyse key aspects of form, structure and language and evaluate perceptively how they shape meanings.	*"Wuthering Heights" is an intricately structured novel of great symmetry. Brontë establishes a powerful dichotomy at the heart of the novel, in which two opposing ways of life interact and conflict with each other. These oppositions are primarily represented by the two houses, Wuthering Heights, which represents nature, and Thrushcross Grange, which represents culture.*
AO3	You show a detailed and perceptive understanding of issues raised through connections between texts and can consider different interpretations with a sharp evaluation of their strengths and weaknesses. You have a range of excellent supportive references.	*Heathcliff's depiction as a doomed and isolated Byronic figure portrays Emily Brontë's engagement with the theme of the soul in torment. This struggle is reflected in Byron's poem "Manfred". There are many similarities between the two texts, not least the anguish felt by both Manfred and Heathcliff at the death of their beloved. However, it could also be argued, as some feminist critics have, that Heathcliff, far from being the archetypal male, is as vulnerable as many of the female characters in this novel, having no property, no income and no name to call his own.*
AO4	You show deep, detailed and relevant understanding of how contextual factors link to the text or task.	*Brontë's fine grasp of the complex inheritance laws of the nineteenth century are crucial to her development of both the plot and characterisation, affecting the key decisions that her female characters make. In spite of Catherine's wild 'wick' ways, when it comes to hard practical socio-economic choices she knows that she has really very little room for manoeuvre, and if she wants freedom, for herself and Heathcliff, she must marry Edgar. Although this choice has been criticised for being in conflict with her true life's passion for Heathcliff, Catherine is correct in her assessment that without Edgar both she and Heathcliff are likely to be left homeless.*

HOW TO WRITE HIGH-QUALITY RESPONSES

The quality of your writing – how you express your ideas – is vital for getting a higher grade, and **AO1** and **AO2** are specifically about **how** you respond.

FIVE KEY AREAS

The quality of your responses can be broken down into five key areas.

1. THE STRUCTURE OF YOUR ANSWER/ESSAY

- First, get **straight to the point or focus in your opening paragraph**. Use a sharp, direct first sentence that deals with a key aspect and then follow up with evidence or detailed reference.
- **Put forward an argument or point of view** (you won't **always** be able to challenge or take issue with the essay question, but generally, where you can, you are more likely to write in an interesting way).
- **Signpost your ideas** with connectives and references which help the essay flow.
- **Don't repeat points already made**, not even in the conclusion, unless you have something new to add.

TARGETING A HIGH GRADE · AO1

Here's an example of an opening paragraph from an essay about the importance of setting that gets straight to the point:

The complex structure of the topography of "Wuthering Heights", which contrasts the two houses and two different landscapes, signals the importance of landscape and setting in Brontë's novel. Brontë uses her descriptions of landscape to symbolic effect. Both the scenery and the weather affect and reflect the characters' moods and actions. At the very beginning of the novel, we are alerted to the significance of the landscape when Lockwood remarks upon the imprisoning effect of the weather:

Immediate focus on task and key words and example from text

> *'A sorrowful sight I saw; dark night coming down prematurely, and sky and hills mingled in one bitter whirl of wind and suffocating snow.'* (p. 14)

The very earth itself becomes confusing, and hostile to human enterprise.

2. USE OF TITLES, NAMES, ETC.

This is a simple, but important, tip to stay on the right side of the examiners.

- Make sure that you spell correctly the titles of the texts, chapters, authors and so on. Present them correctly too, with double quotation marks and capitals as appropriate. For example, "Wuthering Heights".
- Use the **full title**, unless there is a good reason not to (e.g. it's very long).
- Use the term 'text' rather than 'book' or 'story'. If you use the word 'story', the examiner may think you mean the plot/action rather than the 'text' as a whole.

EXAMINER'S TIP ✓

Make sure you know how many marks are available for each **Assessment Objective** in the task you are set. This can help you divide up your time or decide how much attention to give each aspect.

EXAMINER'S TIP ✓

Answer the question set, not the question you'd like to have been asked! Examiners say that often students will be set a question on one aspect (for example, the settings) but end up writing almost as much about another (such as character, e.g. Heathcliff). Or they write about one aspect from the question (for example, 'nightmarish terrors') but ignore another (such as 'dangerous passions'). **Stick to the question**, and answer **all parts of it**.

---

3. EFFECTIVE QUOTATIONS

Do not 'bolt on' quotations to the points you make. You will get some marks for including them, but examiners will not find your writing very fluent.

The best quotations are:

- Relevant
- Not too long
- Integrated into your argument/sentence.

TARGETING A HIGH GRADE — A01

Here is an example of quotations successfully embedded in a sentence:

At the end of the novel Heathcliff's 'single wish' (p. 324) is to be reunited with Catherine; he even feels the 'warm breath' (p. 290) of her ghost after she has died, and the conviction of her continued existence is his guiding force for the next eighteen years.

Remember – quotations can be a well-selected set of three or four single words or phrases embedded in a sentence to build a picture or explanation, or they can be longer ones that are explored and picked apart.

4. TECHNIQUES AND TERMINOLOGY

By all means mention literary terms, techniques, conventions or people (for example, 'paradox' or 'archetype' or 'Eagleton and ideology') **but** make sure that you:

- Understand what they mean
- Are able to link them to what you're saying
- Spell them correctly.

5. GENERAL WRITING SKILLS

Try to write in a way that sounds professional and uses standard English. This does not mean that your writing will lack personality – just that it will be authoritative.

- Avoid colloquial or everyday expressions such as 'got', 'alright', 'ok' and so on.
- Use terms such as 'convey', 'suggest', 'imply', 'infer' to explain the writer's methods.
- Refer to 'we' when discussing the audience/reader.
- Avoid assertions and generalisations; don't just state a general point of view (*Heathcliff is a typical Gothic villain because he's cruel*), but analyse closely with clear evidence and textual detail.

TARGETING A HIGH GRADE — A01

Note the professional approach here:

Brontë's complex exploration of love in this novel identifies a power that is a fundamental driving force of character. Catherine believes that Heathcliff is her guiding principle, her reason for being. As she insists to Nelly Dean, 'my great thought in living is himself' (p. 82). For Brontë, love is all-consuming in terms of identity – for example, Catherine comments: 'Heathcliff is more myself than I am' (p. 82) – and it distorts petty assumptions about what is real, and what is possible. Both Heathcliff and Catherine display a decisive and ultimately obsessive need for each other, and this need drives both their lives and their deaths. As Heathcliff declares: 'My Soul's bliss kills my body, but does not satisfy itself' (p. 333).

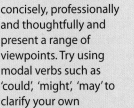

EXAMINER'S TIP

You should comment concisely, professionally and thoughtfully and present a range of viewpoints. Try using modal verbs such as 'could', 'might', 'may' to clarify your own interpretation. For additional help on **Using critical interpretations and perspectives** see pages 98 and 99.

QUESTIONS WITH STATEMENTS, QUOTATIONS OR VIEWPOINTS

One type of question you may come across includes a statement, quotation or viewpoint from another reader.

These questions ask you to respond to, or argue for/against, a specific point of view or critical interpretation.

For *Wuthering Heights* these questions will typically be like this:

- 'In *Wuthering Heights* death is seen as a welcome release from the tortures of living.' How far do you agree with this view of the novel?
- 'Emily Brontë is concerned solely with those primary aspects of life which are unaffected by time and place' (David Cecil, *Early Victorian Novelists*). How far do you agree with this statement?
- To what extent do you agree that '*Wuthering Heights* is about heaven and hell' (Sandra Gilbert, 'Emily Brontë's Bible of Hell')?

The key thing to remember is that you are being asked to **respond to a critical interpretation** of the text – in other words, to come up with **your own 'take'** on the idea or viewpoint in the task.

KEY SKILLS REQUIRED

The table below provides help and advice on answering the question:

How far do you agree that *Wuthering Heights* is 'essentially a love story'?

SKILL	MEANS?	HOW DO I ACHIEVE THIS?
Consider different interpretations	There will be more than one way of looking at the given question. For example, critics might be divided about whether or not *Wuthering Heights* is essentially a love story.	• Show you have considered these different interpretations in your answer. For example: *It is true that one might consider the title to imply that at its heart "Wuthering Heights" is a profound exploration of the nature and properties of love ... Another interpretation is that it has as much to do with revenge as it has to do with love ... A Marxist interpretation would take the view that the love story is subordinate to a social interrogation of the constraints society places upon people's lives and the choices they are able to make ... Feminist critics, such as Sandra Gilbert, have expanded upon this position, arguing that the novel subtly and profoundly challenges our deeply held views about what it means to be feminine and what it means to be masculine.* • Although you may mention different perspectives on the task, you settle on your own view.
Write with a clear, personal voice	Your own 'take' on the question is made obvious to the marker. You are not just repeating other people's ideas, but offering what you think. Although you may mention different perspectives on the task, you settle on your own view.	• Use language that shows careful, but confident, consideration. For example: *Although it has been said that ... I feel that ...*
Construct a coherent argument	The examiner or marker can follow your train of thought so that your own viewpoint is clear to him or her. Write in clear paragraphs that deal logically with different aspects of the question.	• Support what you say with well-selected and relevant evidence. • Use a range of connectives to help 'signpost' your argument. For example, *Expanding upon ... However, such a view fails to take account of ... Notwithstanding the power of this argument, it is important to ...*

ANSWERING A 'VIEWPOINT' QUESTION

Here is an example of a typical question on *Wuthering Heights*:

> **'Brontë presents the opposition of culture and nature in traditionally gendered terms.' To what extent do you agree with this statement?**

STAGE 1: DECODE THE QUESTION

Underline/highlight the **key words**, and make sure you understand what the statement, quote or viewpoint is saying. In this case:

key word/phrases = **opposition** (conflict), **culture**, **nature**, **traditionally gendered** (male/female)

The viewpoint/idea expressed is = Brontë depicts culture and nature as **opposites**, but ones **linked** to the traditional roles of **men** and **women**.

STAGE 2: DECIDE WHAT YOUR VIEWPOINT IS

Examiners have stated that they tend to reward a strong view which is clearly put. Think about the question – can you take issue with it? Disagreeing strongly can lead to higher marks, provided you have **genuine evidence** to support your point of view. Don't disagree just for the sake of it.

STAGE 3: DECIDE HOW TO STRUCTURE YOUR ANSWER

Pick out the key points you wish to make, and decide on the order in which you will present them. Keep this basic plan to hand while you write your response.

STAGE 4: WRITE YOUR RESPONSE

You could start by expanding on the statement or viewpoint expressed in the question.

● For example, in **paragraph 1**:

It could be argued that nature and culture are expressed in culturally gendered terms in "Wuthering Heights", where nature represents the female and culture the male. This alerts us to two important aspects of the novel: its structure and its depiction of the social differences between men and women.

This could help by setting up the various ideas you will choose to explore, argue for/against, and so on. But do not just repeat what the question says or just say what you are going to do. Get straight to the point. For example:

Structurally, "Wuthering Heights" might seem to be a novel which is full of oppositions: male and female, culture and nature, dark and light, outside and inside, civilised and wild, but Brontë's novel seems to interrogate and destabilise these oppositions quite as much as it asserts them.

Then proceed to set out the different arguments or critical perspectives, including your own. This might be done by dealing with specific aspects or elements of the novel one by one. Consider giving 1–2 paragraphs to explore each aspect in turn. Discuss the strengths and weaknesses in each particular point of view. For example:

● **Paragraph 2**: first aspect; **paragraph 3**: a new focus on aspect; **paragraphs 4, 5**, etc. onwards: develop the argument, building a convincing set of points.

● **Last paragraph**: end with a clear statement of your view, without simply listing all the points you have made:

I believe, therefore, that the argument that "Wuthering Heights" presents culture and nature in traditionally gendered terms is only partially correct as there is good evidence to suggest the Brontë saw the distinctions as complex and often blurred …

> **EXAMINER'S TIP** ✓
>
> It is important to clearly signpost ideas through a range of connectives and linking phrases, such as 'However' and 'Turning our attention to …'.

COMPARING *WUTHERING HEIGHTS* WITH OTHER TEXTS

As part of your assessment, you may have to compare *Wuthering Heights* with or link it to other texts that you have studied. These may be other novels, plays or even poetry. You may also have to link or draw in references from texts written by critics. A typical linking or comparison question might be:

> **Compare and contrast the ways in which the breakdown of normal moral and social codes is explored by Emily Brontë in *Wuthering Heights* and in another text you are studying.**

THE TASK

Your task is likely to be on a method, issue, viewpoint or key aspect that is common to *Wuthering Heights* and the other text(s), so you will need to:

Evaluate the issue or statement and have an **open-minded approach**. The best answers suggest meanings and interpretation**s** (plural):

● Do you agree with the statement? Is this aspect more important in one text than in another? Why? How? (Is the theme of 'moral codes breaking down' central or not? What do I understand by this idea anyway?)

● What are the different ways that this question or aspect can be read or viewed?

● Can you challenge this viewpoint? If so, what evidence is there? How can you present it in a thoughtful, reflective way?

Express original or creative approaches fluently:

● This isn't about coming up with entirely new ideas, but you need to show that you're actively engaged with thinking about the question and are not just reeling off things you have learned.

● **Synthesise** your ideas – pull ideas and points together to create something fresh.

● This is a linking/comparison response, so ensure that you guide your reader through your ideas logically, clearly and with professional language.

Know what to compare/contrast: form, structure and **language** will **always** be central to your response, even where you also have to write about characters, contexts or culture.

● Think about: dual versus more conventional narration, reported speech, diaries, repetitions, time frames or narrative voice which leads to dislocation or difficulty in reading.

● Consider different characteristic uses of language: lengths of sentences, formal/informal style, dialect, accent, balance of dialogue and narration, texts within texts, sub-clauses.

● Look at a variety of symbols, images, motifs (how they represent concerns of the author/time; what they are and how and where they appear; how they link to critical perspectives; their purposes, effects and impact on the novel).

● Consider aspects of genres (to what extent do Brontë and the author of the other work conform to/challenge/ subvert particular genres or styles of writing?).

WRITING YOUR RESPONSE

The depth and extent of your answer will depend on how much you have to write, but the key will be to **explore in detail**, and **link between ideas and texts**. Let us use the same example:

Compare and contrast the ways in which the breakdown of normal moral and social codes is explored by Emily Brontë in *Wuthering Heights* and in another text you are studying.

INTRODUCTION TO YOUR RESPONSE

- Discuss quickly what 'normal moral and social codes' are, and how well this concept applies to your texts. You may wish to draw on classical, everyday or literary definitions, but only do so briefly.

- Briefly mention, in support, evidence that some sorts of 'moral codes' one might expect to find in *Wuthering Heights* could be seen as 'broken'.

- You could begin with a powerful quotation that you use to launch into your response. For example:

> *'"You were very wicked, Mr Heathcliff!" I exclaimed; "were you not ashamed to disturb the dead?"*
>
> *"I disturbed nobody, Nelly," he replied; "and I gave some ease to myself."' (p. 289) In this quotation we clearly see that Heathcliff sets himself outside usual moral codes, in a manner that reflects William Blake's fervent opposition to institutionalised religion and the oppressive moral laws it promoted, as outlined for example in Blake's "Proverbs of Hell".*

MAIN BODY OF YOUR RESPONSE

- Point 1: start with the 'moral and social codes' in *Wuthering Heights* and what they imply about society. What is your view? Are the moral/social codes similar in the other text? What do the critics say? Whose views will you use? Are there contextual/cultural factors to consider?

- Point 2: now cover a new factor or aspect through comparison or contrast of the breaking of moral codes in *Wuthering Heights* with another in a second text. How is the breakdown of codes in this text presented **differently or similarly** by the writer according to language, form, structures used; why was this done in this way? What do the critics say? Are there contextual/cultural factors to consider?

- Points 3, 4, 5, etc.: address a range of other factors and aspects, for example other types of moral/social codes, or other characters or narrative routes that represent them, **either** within *Wuthering Heights* **or** in both *Wuthering Heights* and another text. What different ways do you respond to these (with more empathy, greater criticism, less interest?) – and why?

> *Catherine's response to Heathcliff's marriage to Isabella Linton is hard-headed in its description of Heathcliff's amoral motivations: '"I know he couldn't love a Linton; and yet, he'd be quite capable of marrying your fortune and expectations. Avarice is growing with him a besetting sin."' (p. 103).*

CONCLUSION

- Synthesise elements of what you have said into a final paragraph that fluently, succinctly and inventively leaves the reader/examiner with the sense that you have engaged with this task and the texts.

> *In conclusion, it can be seen that both Brontë and Blake establish a new version of morality, having at the heart of their work an authentic sense of good and evil that is not socially constrained but which is robustly defended through character. It is not simply what we do that makes us good or evil, it is who we are.*

EXAMINER'S TIP

Be creative with your conclusion! It's the last thing the examiner will read and your chance to make your mark.

EXAMINER'S TIP ✓

You may be asked to discuss other texts you have studied as well as *Wuthering Heights* as part of your response. Once you have completed your response on the novel you could move on to discuss the same issues in your other texts. Begin with a simple linking phrase or sentence to launch straight into your first point about your next text, such as:

'The same issue/idea is explored in a quite different way in [name of text] … Here, …

RESPONDING TO A GENERAL QUESTION ABOUT THE WHOLE TEXT

You may also be asked to write about a specific aspect of *Wuthering Heights* – but as it relates to the **whole text**. For example:

> **Explore the ways in which Brontë uses different settings in *Wuthering Heights* to contribute to the Gothic effects of the novel.**

This means you should:

- Focus on *both* the settings *and* their Gothic effects
- Explain *how* **Brontë uses them** – *how* they are used to construct ideas about morality and monstrosity, how they add strangeness and disturbance, and how they unsettle our reading of the love story
- Look at aspects of the **whole novel**, not just one part of it

STRUCTURING YOUR RESPONSE

You need a clear, logical plan, as for all tasks that you do. It is impossible to write about every section or part of the text, so you will need to:

- Quickly note 5–6 key points or aspects to build your essay around, e.g.

Point a: Features of the Gothic include: ghosts, ancient buildings, graveyards. Wuthering Heights can be considered part of the domestic Gothic.

Point b: Gothic signifies writing of excess: the disturbing return of the past upon the present. *Wuthering Heights* is a novel of excessive emotions and behaviour, where time is constantly shifting. Supernatural versus natural causes.

Point c: Gothic landscapes are alienating and full of menace (Lockwood's account of the landscape and environment).

Point d: In Gothic novels imagination exceeds reason, and passion and powerful emotion are set against rational knowledge and conventional comprehension (relationship between Heathcliff and Catherine).

Point e: Gothic fictions seem to promote vice and violence, being anti-religious, and giving free rein to self-seeking ambition (Heathcliff's plan for revenge).

- Then decide the most effective or logical order. For example, **point c, then b, a, d, e**, etc.

You could begin with your key or main idea, with supporting evidence/references, followed by your further points (perhaps two paragraphs for each). For example:

Paragraph 1: first key point: *With its uncanny disruptions of the boundaries between inside and outside, and its doubling of names and identities, "Wuthering Heights" can be considered in very many ways typical of the Gothic genre.*

Paragraph 2: expand out, link into other areas: *This is also marked in Lockwood's experience of the landscape, which he describes as 'sky and hills mingled in one bitter whirl of wind and suffocating snow' (p. 14).*

Paragraph 3: change direction, introduce new aspect/point: *Imaginative excess marks the novel in a number of profound ways: Heathcliff's mounting violence, which culminates in his opening of Catherine's grave to lie with her, and his refusal of traditional religious values can all be read as part of a Gothic enterprise.* And so on.

EXAMINER'S TIP ✓

Use a compelling way to finish, perhaps repeating some or all of the key words from the question. For example, you could end with your final point, but **add a last clause** which makes it clear what you think is key to the question: *In conclusion, the effect of such potent Gothic imagery in the novel is to unsettle long-held assumptions about what is 'natural' and right, and beyond question.*

Or you could end with a **new quotation** or an **aspect** that's **slightly different from** your main point: *Finally, as Fred Botting says in his analysis of the historical transformations of Gothic literature: "Tyranny and horror are both nightmarish and real ... "* (p. 127).

Or, of course, you can combine these endings.

WRITING ABOUT CONTEXTS

Assessment Objective 4 asks you to 'demonstrate understanding of the significance and influence of the contexts in which literary texts are written and received ...'. This can mean:

● How the events, settings, politics and so on **of the time when the text was written** influenced the writer or help us to understand the novel's themes or concerns. For example, to what extent might Brontë have been influenced by the death of her mother, and the overshadowing prevalence of fatal disease in Victorian England, in her account of her female characters in *Wuthering Heights*?

or

● How events, settings, politics and so on **of the time when the text is read or seen** influence how it is understood. For example, would the very early readers of the novel have seen it differently, believing that it was written by a man, and so on?

THE CONTEXT FOR *WUTHERING HEIGHTS*

You might find the following table helpful for thinking about how particular aspects of the time contribute to our understanding of the novel and its themes. There are just examples – can you think of any others?

POLITICAL	LITERARY	PHILOSOPHICAL
1834 Parish workhouses introduced Abolition of slavery in territories governed by Britain	**1816–17** Lord Byron: *Manfred* **1818** Mary Shelley: *Frankenstein*; Lord Byron: *Childe Harold*	**1859** John Stuart Mill: *On Liberty* **1832** Jeremy Bentham, founder of Utilitarianism, dies
SCIENTIFIC	CULTURAL	SOCIAL
1821 Faraday invents first electric engine **1859** Charles Darwin: *The Origin of Species*	**1780 –1850** Second Industrial Revolution **1830** Liverpool and Manchester Railway built	**1875** Public Health Plan **1811** Luddite riots, Nottingham

TARGETING A HIGH GRADE

Remember that the extent to which you write about these contexts will be determined by the marks available. Some questions or tasks may have very few marks allocated for **AO4**, but where you do have to refer to context the key thing is **not** to 'bolt on' your comments, or write a long, separate chunk of text on context and then 'go back' to the novel.

For example:

Don't just write:

Emily Brontë had an extensive and detailed knowledge of the law. She was very interested in the inheritance laws of the nineteenth century, and also the laws which exempted clergy from prosecution for certain crimes. This was perhaps in response to her own position as a woman in society, because the law in the nineteenth century favoured men over women. The influence of this can be seen in how Emily Brontë developed her plot, giving Heathcliff ownership of both properties in the end.

Do write:

Essential to the plot-line of "Wuthering Heights" is an understanding of the intricacies of the inheritance laws of the nineteenth century. Not only is it integral to the plot, but it also affects how we perceive character, for very often it is the character of Nelly Dean who makes references to the legal niceties, thus providing an argument for a reading of her grasp of the situation as not merely instinctive but both sophisticated and informed.

EXAMINER'S TIP ✓

Remember that linking the historical, literary or social context to the novel itself is key to achieving the best marks for AO4.

USING CRITICAL INTERPRETATIONS AND PERSPECTIVES

THE 'MEANING' OF A TEXT

There are many viewpoints and perspectives on the 'meaning' of *Wuthering Heights*, and examiners will be looking for evidence that you have considered a range of these. Broadly speaking, these different interpretations might relate to:

1. CHARACTER

What **sort/type** of person Heathcliff – or another character – is:

● Is the character an 'archetype' (a specific type of character with common features)? Sandra Gilbert in her essay 'Emily Brontë's Bible of Hell' offers a **psychoanalytic** view of Heathcliff, seeing him as completing an 'alternative self, or double' for Catherine. He could also be read as an archetypal **Romantic** villain, or a **Byronic hero**.

● Does the character personify, symbolise or represent a specific idea or trope (the psychologically tormented; the **Gothic** 'Other' or 'Double')?

● Is the character modern, universal, of his/her time, historically accurate, etc.? (For example, can we see aspects of today's romantic heroes in Heathcliff? How does he link/ connect with the Byronic hero?)

2. IDEAS AND ISSUES

What the novel tells us about **particular ideas** or **issues** and how we can interpret these. For example:

● How society is constructed
● The role of men/women
● What the Gothic means
● Moral and social codes.

3. LINKS AND CONTEXTS

To what extent the novel **links with**, **follows** or **pre-echoes** other texts and/or ideas. For example:

● Its influence culturally, historically and socially: do we see echoes of the settings, contexts or genres in other texts? (For example, the Brontës were all familiar with the works of Shakespeare, and there are many parallels between this novel and Shakepeare's tragedies, notably *Hamlet* and *King Lear*.)

● How its language links to other texts or modes, such as religious works, myth, legend.

4. NARRATIVE STRUCTURE

How the novel is **constructed** and how Brontë **makes** her narrative:

● Does it follow particular narrative conventions?
● What is the function of specific events, characters, plot devices, locations, etc. in relation to narrative?
● What are the specific moments of tension, conflict, crisis and denouement?

5. READER RESPONSE

How the novel **works on a reader**, and whether this changes over time and in different contexts:

● How does Brontë **position** the reader? Are we to empathise with, feel distance from, judge and/or evaluate the events and characters?

And finally, how different readers view the novel: for example, different readers in Victorian, postwar or more recent times.

CHECK THE BOOK A03

The novel has many dramatic features: its central concern with order and disorder, Heathcliff's unknown origins, and the story arc through tragedy to happy resolution are all elements which would be familiar to readers of Shakespeare, and some of the monologues resemble stage soliloquies in their dramatic effect. Also Sir Walter Scott's influence upon the novel can be seen to be extensive. The character of Heathcliff owes a great deal to Rashleigh Osbaldistone in *Rob Roy*, and many of the landscape descriptions in *Rob Roy* find their echo in *Wuthering Heights*.

WRITING ABOUT CRITICAL PERSPECTIVES

The important thing to remember is that you are a critic too. Your job is to evaluate what a critic or school of criticism has said about the elements above, and arrive at your own conclusions. In essence, you need to: **consider** the views of others, **synthesise** them, then decide on **your perspective**. For example:

EXPLAIN THE VIEWPOINTS

Critical view A about power in *Wuthering Heights*:

> *Feminist readings have contrasted the characterisation of Heathcliff and Edgar Linton in terms of power. Sandra Gilbert offers an intriguing reading of Heathcliff as 'feminine' because he lacks cultural power.*

Critical view B about power in *Wuthering Heights*:

> *Terry Eagleton's Marxist analysis of power in "Wuthering Heights" also focuses on the choice that Catherine makes between Heathcliff and Edgar Linton, and sees the choice in terms of ideology. Catherine's choice is not made from love, Eagleton argues, but from an understanding of social power relations.*

THEN SYNTHESISE AND ADD YOUR PERSPECTIVE

> *The idea that Heathcliff has no 'masculine' power, as expressed by Sandra Gilbert, can be contrasted with Terry Eagleton's comment that 'In a crucial act of self-betrayal and bad faith, Catherine rejects Heathcliff as a suitor because he is socially inferior to Linton – Eagleton sees Heathcliff's lack of power not in psycho-sexual terms but as socially produced.*
>
> *However, I feel that both these readings fail to take into account the fact that Heathcliff occupies the most powerful thematic position in the novel. Heathcliff is essential to the development of both the major themes of the novel: love and revenge. The power of his love for Catherine is one which can summon her from the grave, and thus is one which extends beyond death. His power over Isabella, Hindley, Linton and, to a certain extent, Hareton enables him to implement his complex plan for revenge. So it can be seen that in spite of convincing arguments to the contrary, without Heathcliff this novel would be distinctly lacking in power and thematic purpose.*

TARGETING A HIGH GRADE (A03)

Make sure you have thoroughly explored the different types of criticism written about *Wuthering Heights*. Critical interpretation of novels can range from reviews and comments written about the text at the time that it was first published through to critical analysis by a modern critic or reader writing today. Bear in mind that views of texts can change over time as values and experiences themselves change, and that criticism can be written for different purposes.

CRITICAL VIEWPOINT A03

C. P. Sanger's reading of the novel's structure (1926) was at pains to distance the novel from some of the moral criticism it had received during its early reviews. Sanger paid attention to the formal aspects of the novel, arguing that the symmetry of the family relationships, and the whole intricate structure of the novel, redeemed it from its initial reception as 'a fiend of a book, a monster'. Sanger's critique can be seen as paving the way for critics such as Mark Schorer (1949), who investigated the patterns of imagery in the text.

CRITICAL VIEWPOINT A03

More contemporary critics such as Hillis Miller (1982) also focus on the structure of *Wuthering Heights*, but see the repetitions and symmetry as deferring stable meanings, leaving any firm conclusions about this novel and what it might mean tantalisingly out of reach.

ANNOTATED SAMPLE ANSWERS

Below are extracts from two sample answers to the same question at different grades. Bear in mind that these are examples only, covering all four Assessment Objectives – you will need to check the type of question and the weighting given for the AOs when writing your coursework essay or practising for your exam.

> **Question: Consider the use and effect of nature imagery in *Wuthering Heights*.**

CANDIDATE 1

AO2 — A quotation would have helped here, ideally with language analysis

Emily Brontë uses a great deal of nature imagery in "Wuthering Heights". Indeed, in the first sentence of the novel we are told by Lockwood as he returns from his first visit to Wuthering Heights that the countryside is beautiful. The setting of Wuthering Heights, on the bleak moors of Yorkshire, is essential to our appreciation of the novel. In the second chapter the descriptions change as the weather becomes more hostile. 'One may guess the power of the north wind, blowing over the edge, by the excessive slant of a few stunted firs at the end of the house; and by a range of gaunt thorns all stretching their limbs one way, as of craving the alms of the sun' (p.4). This has the effect of making us realise that we are in a real place. The realistic description of the setting is juxtaposed with the surreal aspects of this novel, such as ghosts, to make the reader uncertain about what is real and what is not. This emphasis on nature imagery also indicates the time in which Brontë was writing, when a largely rural lifestyle was under threat from industrialisation.

AO2 — Consideration of language but no sustained analysis of quotation and no exploration of the emotional effect of the imagery

AO4 — Good introduction of context, should be picked up again later

Brontë uses a lot of animal imagery in her novel, and Lockwood's mistake when he identifies some dead rabbits as cats means that his narrative is unreliable. His description of himself as 'feeble as a kitten' can be related to this. Many of the other characters are described in natural terms, as animals. This indicates that they are wild and uncivilised people. It also might indicate other qualities in their characters, such as when Hareton is described as a cart-horse and taunted about whether he ever dreams. This tells us that Hareton works hard and belongs on the land, but is untroubled by an imagination. It also connects with one of the main themes of the novel which is dreams.

AO2 — Good point but unclearly expressed. Could be developed further

AO1 — Simplistic analysis, which shows insufficient knowledge of the text. Provide brief examples

AO2 — Shows how Bronte uses imagery to reveal character; also demonstrates an understanding of the wider implications for the novel's central themes

Brontë lived in the landscape she describes so she has a good knowledge of the flowers and the moors, which she describes in great detail in all sorts of weather. This shows time passing, which is important for the plot. Also she describes the people as flowers and trees showing how close to nature they are. This is important because Brontë uses the natural world to describe a new version of Heaven, a Heaven that can be experienced on earth. This would have been quite a shocking idea to her

AO1 — Good point clumsily made

AO2 — This point needs to be supported with an example from the text and the analysis needs to be developed more thoroughly

A03 Good exploration of contemporary readers' reaction

A01 Good point, rather clumsily made

readership, since in the nineteenth century it was believed that Heaven was a place you aspired to after death, and it was part of what helped you to live a moral life.

Another way in which Brontë uses nature imagery is in her symbolic use of weather. The weather is portrayed as a great force, which the characters are at the mercy of. The weather comes then to symbolise the themes of the novel, like love and revenge, which are also great forces over which the characters have no control. Not only does it signify the themes of the novel, it also signifies character. Catherine and Heathcliff love being out on the moor more than anything, and likewise their personalities are considered wild and untamed.

A03 Supporting critical quotation would have helped make this point more strongly

GRADE C

Comment

This answer shows some knowledge of the text (A01), but the points are insufficiently developed or supported by quotation. The candidate finds a number of examples of nature imagery, but often fails to consider what their effect might be (A02). There is some helpful awareness of how Victorian readers responded to the text (AO3) but this could have been developed further, as could the reference to industrialisation (AO4).

For a B grade

- A greater use of embedded quotations would have enhanced this essay
- The points need to be developed further and supported by critical analysis and further discussion of relevant contexts

CANDIDATE 2

A01 Articulate and relevant response using correct literary terminology

Emily Brontë's deployment of nature imagery in "Wuthering Heights" is absolutely central to the novel and works on a number of levels. On one level the images are metaphoric: when Catherine describes her love of Edgar Linton as being like the 'foliage in the woods. Time will change it, I'm well aware, as winter changes the trees' (p. 82). This is an interesting moment in the novel. Catherine does not compare Edgar himself to the foliage, but rather her love for him. Leaves do not 'change' in the winter, but die; so this passage can be seen as a subtle intimation that Catherine knows that her love for Edgar will die. The foliage, therefore, symbolises her love for Edgar which is not eternal, but which is flowering at this point in the novel.

A02 Good choice of quotation

A01 Excellent awareness of the novel as a whole

By contrast Catherine describes her love for Heathcliff as resembling 'the eternal rocks beneath' (p. 82). The imagery here suggests that her love for Heathcliff is elemental and fundamental. Such descriptions also affect our understanding of character. Catherine and Heathcliff are at their happiest out on the moors, and their characters are both wild and flinty. Lockwood, in a rare moment of insight, describes it thus: '[The] people in these regions ... do live more in earnest, more in themselves, and less in surface change, and frivolous external things' (p. 62).

A01 Original use of language

Another way in which Brontë uses the imagery of the rocks is symbolic: when Cathy describes Penistone Craggs to Nelly as 'golden' and 'bright' (p. 190) they represent for her the brilliant appeal of the unknown. The crags really exist, and they symbolise a life beyond the confines of Thrushcross Grange. Thus it can be seen that the imagery works both symbolically and metaphorically, and is an essential tool for Brontë in telling her narrative. It must also be remembered that much of the natural environment described in the novel was Brontë's own and we may attribute Cathy and Catherine's passion for the landscape to Brontë's own love for the natural world and her desire to preserve it.

A02 Excellent sustained exploration

A04 Good use of contextual detail could be further developed

Some of the most striking natural images in the novel have to do with animals. Throughout the novel Brontë uses animals to denote human characteristics. Isabella is likened to a 'canary' (p. 102) but she is also called a 'tigress' only a few pages later. Isabella may well be a 'tame bird' in Catherine's eyes, but she is capable of great cruelty herself. This is important, for it informs our response to Heathcliff's cruelty to Isabella later on. A feminist reading of this might see the contradictions between the canary and the tigress in Isabella's character as representative of the conflict for women in society. Although they are required by convention to appear as merely decorative birds, their true natures are more complex, encompassing the wilder protective instincts of the tigress. Indeed, in the space of a few pages; Isabella is referred to as a monkey, a vixen, a canary, a tigress, a centipede, a dove and an angel. Other instances of bird imagery include a reference to Hareton as an 'unfledged dunnock' by Nelly, which is suggestive both of his

A03 Interesting critical analysis of the use of the imagery

entrapment by Heathcliff, and of his wildness in comparison to the domestic reference to a canary.

AO2 Excellent analysis

A recurrent use of animal imagery can also be seen in the way in which Brontë uses references to dogs in "Wuthering Heights". When Catherine is savaged by the guard dog at Thrushcross Grange, the dog represents the brutal lengths to which civilisation will go to protect its property. The Marxist critic Terry Eagleton sees this as an example of the violence at the heart of capitalism. Later in the novel Cathy's two pointers are mauled by the wilder dogs at the Heights. The conflict between civilised and savage characters in the novel is closely mirrored by a series of incidents involving tame and wild animals.

AO3 Interesting use of supportive critical material

Another effect of the nature imagery in "Wuthering Heights" is to imbue the novel with the sense of time passing in relation to the seasons. This is significant because it also symbolises the shifting mood and tone of the novel This relationship between the weather and the action of the novel is known as a pathetic fallacy. Appropriate use of literary term. The fact that the weather and landscape are often perceived to be hostile to the inhabitants frequently demonstrates their social as well as physical vulnerability, as when Lockwood is trapped by the snow. 'A sorrowful sight I saw; dark night coming down prematurely, and sky and hills mingled in one bitter whirl of wind and suffocating snow' (p. 14). All in all, therefore, I would suggest that Brontë's use of nature imagery runs through many layers of the novel, affecting characters and readers alike, to become an essential part of what it is to experience "Wuthering Heights".

AO2 Appropriate use of literary term

AO1 A convincing and personal conclusion

GRADE A

Comment
This is a thorough and sensitive answer to the question. It is well expressed (AO1) and a good range of literary techniques is mentioned (AO2). Textual knowledge is excellent and there are some perceptive comments and well-chosen quotations. The requirements of the question are kept in the foreground at all times. The essay makes reference to other critical interpretations of the text and uses them appropriately (AO3), while the author's love of nature is also alluded to (AO4).

For an A* grade
- An approach which compared and evaluated different critical positions in relation to the question would have gained a higher grade
- Reference to other works of literature with which Brontë was familiar would suggest parallels and contrasts, and further contextualisation would also have enhanced the grade

WORKING THROUGH A TASK

Now it's your turn to work through a task on *Wuthering Heights*. The key is to:

- Read/decode the task/question
- Plan your points – then expand and link your points
- Draft your answer

TASK TITLE

'In *Wuthering Heights* death is seen as a welcome release from the tortures of living.' How far do you agree with this view of the novel?

DECODE THE QUESTION: KEY WORDS

How far do you agree ...?	= I need to judge how true this viewpoint is
death is ... a welcome release	= characters' deaths provide a happy escape
tortures of living	= real life is painful, cruel and full of despair

PLAN AND EXPAND

- Key aspect: evidence of death as a welcome release

POINT	EXPANDED POINT	EVIDENCE
Point a *Death a central motif. Heathcliff's single wish to join Catherine in the grave (p. 324).*	*This can be related back to Catherine's declaration that she and Heathcliff are the same. When she is dead, Heathcliff is doomed to live a spiritually diminished life. Heathcliff is tortured by visions and memories of Catherine, to the point where even revenge loses its savour.* *This is a question which engages profoundly with Emily Brontë's re-imagining of heaven in this novel, which she figures as a 'heaven on earth'. Sandra Gilbert's essay 'Emily Brontë's Bible of Hell' argues that this is a novel which raises questions about heaven and hell more urgently than any other English novel.*	*'I have neither a fear, nor a presentiment, nor a hope of death – why should I?'* (p. 324) *'My Soul's bliss kills my body, but does not satisfy itself'* (p. 333)
Point b *Heathcliff by no means the only character to feel that death is a welcome release. Isabella's thoughts too turn to the grave when her marriage to Heathcliff deteriorates (p. 175).*	Different aspects of this point expanded *You fill in*	Quotations 1–2 *You fill in*
Point c *Catherine's 'blessed release' (p. 167) queried by Nelly.*	Different aspects of this point expanded *You fill in*	Quotations 1–2 *You fill in*

- Key aspect: evidence of real life being painful

You come up with three points, and then expand them

POINT	EXPANDED POINT	EVIDENCE
Point a *You fill in*	Different aspect of this point expanded *You fill in*	Quotations 1–2 *You fill in*
Point b *You fill in*	Different aspects of this point expanded *You fill in*	Quotations 1–2 *You fill in*
Point c *You fill in*	Different aspects of this point expanded *You fill in*	Quotations 1–2 *You fill in*

CONCLUSION

POINT	EXPANDED POINT	EVIDENCE
Key final point or overall view *You fill in*	Draw together and perhaps add a final further point to support your view *You fill in*	Final quotation to support your view *You fill in*

DEVELOP FURTHER AND DRAFT

Now look back over your draft points and:

- Add further links or connections between the points to develop them further or synthesise what has been said, for example:

> *When Catherine dies Nelly announces her death as a 'blessed release'. However, while it may be true that death is something Catherine has yearned for and even initiated, the fact that after her death she haunts Heathcliff, and is not at peace, suggests that her death has in no conventional sense of the term been a blessed, or welcome, release from the torment of living.*

- Decide an order for your points/paragraphs – some may now be linked/connected and therefore **not** in the order of the table above.

Now draft your essay. If you're really stuck you can use the opening paragraph below to get you started.

> *Death is a central motif in "Wuthering Heights", and our understanding of its significance is key to our understanding of the novel. From Mr Earnshaw's death in Volume I, Chapter V, through to Heathcliff's 'girnning at death' in Volume II, Chapter XX, death marks everyone in the novel. From laws of inheritance to constructions of paradise, death is an unavoidable reality in this novel. The longing for a death that rejected conventional views of heaven in favour of a paradise that was as similar to earth as possible was an idea that was central to Brontë's writing in her poetry and throughout the narrative. In this way, we see that …*

Once you've written your essay, turn to page 112 for a mark scheme on this question to see how well you've done.

ESSENTIAL STUDY TOOLS

FURTHER QUESTIONS

1) Consider the use of symbolism in *Wuthering Heights*.

2) How does Emily Brontë retain the reader's sympathy for Heathcliff, in spite of his increasingly demonic behaviour?

3) To what extent can Heathcliff be considered a Byronic hero?

4) How far do you agree with the description of *Wuthering Heights* as one of the world's greatest love stories?

5) How does Brontë make use of Gothic conventions in this novel, and to what effect?

6) Does Cathy's story reverse or repeat her mother's and to what effect?

7) How effective is the device of dual narration in *Wuthering Heights*?

8) Consider Brontë's use of time in this novel.

9) How important are dreams in this novel?

10) Compare and contrast the characters of Heathcliff and Edgar with reference to one of the following: tragedy, masculinity, authenticity.

11) Compare and contrast the two houses, Wuthering Heights and Thrushcross Grange, with reference to two of the following: violence, knowledge, home, charity.

12) Compare and contrast the different views of faith and religion depicted in this novel.

FURTHER READING

THE TEXT

Linda H. Peterson, ed., *Wuthering Heights: Case Studies in Contemporary Criticism*, Bedford Books of St Martin's Press, 1992
The complete text with five critical essays, an introduction to the context and a survey of critical responses. This is thorough and very useful.

Emily Brontë, *The Complete Poems*, ed. Derek Roper with Edward Chitham, Clarendon Press, 1995
Very useful to compare some of the themes in the poetry with the themes of the novel.

BIOGRAPHY

Juliet Barker, *The Brontës*, Weidenfield & Nicholson, 1994, reprinted 2010
A clear and passionate biography of the family.

Trevor J. Barnes and James S. Duncan, eds, *Writing Worlds: Discourse, Text and Metaphor*, Routledge & Kegan Paul, 1992

Lord David Cecil, *Early Victorian Novelists: Essays in Revaluation*, revised edition, University of Chicago Press, 1958; originally published 1935

Jay Clayton, *Romantic Vision and The Novel*, Cambridge University Press, 1987.

Elizabeth Gaskell, *The Life of Charlotte Brontë*, Smith, Elder & Co., London, 1857; reprinted by Penguin Books, 1975
The first published biography of one of the Brontë sisters.

Winifred Gérin, *Emily Brontë*, Clarendon Press, 1971
Clear and insightful biography.

Katherine Frank, *Emily Brontë: A Chainless Soul*, H. Hamilton, 1990, paperback, Penguin Books, Harmondsworth, 1992
Interesting new interpretation of Brontë's life which draws on issues of social isolation and self-denial.

A. Mary F. Robinson, *Emily Brontë*, W.H. Allen, 1883
Early biography of Emily Brontë.

CRITICAL WORKS

Miriam Allott, ed., *Emily Brontë: Wuthering Heights: A Selection of Critical Essays*, Macmillan, 1970
An authoritative collection of essays.

Nancy Armstrong, 'Imperialist Nostalgia and *Wuthering Heights*', in Linda H. Peterson, ed., *Wuthering Heights: Case Studies in Contemporary Criticism*, 1992
An influential essay in this excellent collection.

Harold Bloom, ed., *Emily Brontë's Wuthering Heights,* Chelsea, 1987
Useful and wide-ranging collection of essays.

Ian Brinton, *Brontë's Wuthering Heights: Readers Guides*, Continuum International Publishing Group, 2010
A clear and well-written guide to reading the text.

Lord David Cecil, *Early Victorian Novelists: Essays in Revaluation*, revised edition, University of Chicago Press, 1958; originally published 1935
An early collection of essays.

Sydney Dobell, 'Currer Bell and *Wuthering Heights*', Palladium (September 1850)
Early critical response to the novel.

Terry Eagleton, *Myths of Power: A Marxist Study of the Brontës*, Harper & Row, 1975, 2nd edition, Macmillan, 1992
An important Marxist reading of the works of the Brontës.

Eva Figes, *Sex and Subterfuge, Women Writers in 1850*, Pandora, 1982
An interesting feminist account of Victorian women writers.

Juliann E. Fleenor, ed., *The Female Gothic*, Eden Press, 1983
A useful account of how women writers have adapted the Gothic genre.

Sigmund Freud, *The Interpretation of Dreams*, Penguin; first Penguin edition 1953
Essential reading for an understanding of psychoanalytical criticism and useful for intereapreting the dream passages in *Wuthering Heights*.

Sandra Gilbert and Susan Gubar, *The Madwoman in the Attic: The Woman Writer and the Nineteenth-Century Literary Imagination*, Yale University Press, 1979
Influential feminist reading of Victorian women writers.

Margaret Homans, 'Dreaming of Children: Literalization in *Jane Eyre* and *Wuthering Heights*', in Juliann E. Fleenor, ed., *The Female Gothic*, Eden Press, 1983 (see above)

E. Jolly, ed., *The Life and Letters of Sydney Dobell*, volume 1, Smith, 1878

Frank Kermode, *The Classic*, Faber & Faber, 1975

Robert Kiely, *The Romantic Novel in England*, Harvard University Press, 1972

Nicholas Marsh, *Emily Brontë: Wuthering Heights*, Analysing Texts, Macmillan, 1999
A useful guide to analysing the novel.

J. Hillis Miller, *Fiction and Repetition*, Harvard University Press and Basil Blackwell, 1982
Important deconstructive reading of the novel.

Sara Mills, Lynne Pearce, Susan Spaull, Elaine Millard, eds, *Feminist Readings, Feminists Reading*, Harvester Wheatsheaf, 1989

Ruth Robbins, *Literary Feminisms*, Macmillan, 2000
Clear introduction to feminist literary theory.

Rick Rylance, ed., *Debating Texts*, OUP, 1987

C. P. Sanger, *The Structure of 'Wuthering Heights'*, Hogarth Press, 1926
Influential and important structuralist reading of the novel.

Mark Schorer, 'Fiction and the Matrix of Analogy', *The Kenyon Review* 11:4 (Autumn 1949)

Susan Sontag, *Illness as Metaphor and Aids and its Metaphors*, Penguin, 1991

Patsy Stoneman, ed., *Wuthering Heights: Contemporary Critical Essays*, Macmillan, 1993
Important collection of critical essays.

Julia Swindells, *Victorian Writing and Working Women*, University of Minnesota Press, 1985
An interesting contextual account of Victorian women writers.

Dorothy Van Ghent, *The English Novel: Form and Function*, Harper Torchbooks, 1961
Influential analysis of the novel.

Marina Warner, *From the Beast to the Blonde*, Chatto & Windus, 1994

Raymond Williams, *The Country and the City*, Chatto & Windus, 1973

Philip K. Wion, 'The Absent Mother in Emily Brontë's *Wuthering Heights*', *American Imago* 42 (1985)

LITERARY TERMS

anecdote secret or unpublished narratives; the narrative of a striking event; from 1761, an item of gossip

archetype a standard character type showing typical traits, e.g. the vampire, the hero.

biographial criticism a critical approach which focuses upon the relationship between fiction and reality by drawing upon the author's life-story

Byronic hero characteristically both glamorous and dangerous, haunted by the guilt of mysterious crimes

deconstruction a **post-structuralist** approach to literature initiated by the theoretical ideas of Jacques Derrida. Deconstruction posits the radical undecidability of all texts

deconstructive see **deconstruction**, adjective pertaining to the term

destabilising to make uncertain, to unsettle meaning

discourse discourse theory is associated with the writings of Michel Foucault. Discourse generally refers to the language in which a specific area of knowledge is discussed, e.g. the discourse of law or medicine

eponymous relating to or being the person or thing after which something is named

feminist criticism there are many different forms of feminist criticism: some critics suggest ways of reading which draw attention to the patriarchal assumptions underpinning cultural production; others focus on the rediscovery of works by women writers; still others concentrate on the psychological and linguistic opportunities for women in a male-dominated culture

formalism also known as **new criticism**; formalists concentrate on the formal structure of the text, particularly such elements as imagery, symbolism, repetition

frame narrative a story that encloses another story

Gothic a genre of writing which has a number of typical elements such ghosts, horror, sublime landscapes

gynocriticism a term which refers to the practice of turning away from the analysis of male-authored texts to an analysis of female-authored texts and their specific differences from one another

hegemony associated with the political writings of Antonio Gramsci, hegemony refers to the web of ideologies that shape people's view of the world

hermeneutics the art or science of interpretation

ideology a set of beliefs about the world which seems both natural and inevitable.

Marxist criticism a way of reading texts that focuses upon their material and historical conditions

metaphor a figure of speech in which a word or phase is applied to an object, a character or an action which does not literally belong to it, in order to imply a resemblance and create an unusual or striking image in the reader's mind

metaphysical visionary writing, generally associated with the seventeenth century; incorporeal, abstract

narrative a story, tale or any recital of events, and the manner in which it is told. First person narratives ('I') are told from the character's perspective and usually require the reader to judge carefully what is being said; second person **narratives** ('you') suggest the reader is part of the story; in third person narratives ('he', 'she', 'they'), the **narrator** may be intrusive (continually commenting on the story), impersonal or **omniscient**. More than one style or narrative may be used in a text.

narrator the voice telling the story or relating a sequence of events

new criticism see **formalism**

new historicism a form of criticism heavily influenced by Marxist criticism and the work of Michel Foucault. Foucault's notions of 'power' and 'discourse' were particularly formative of new historicist thinking.

novel of manners late eighteenth-century literary genre which deals with the conflict between individual aspirations and the accepted codes of social behaviour. There is a vital relationship between social behaviour, manners and character. Manners have a moral value, as well as a social value in this genre

omniscient narrator a narrator who uses the third person narrative and has an overarching knowledge of events and of the thoughts and feelings of the characters

palimpsest a text that is overwritten with other narratives and messages

parable a story which explains something that cannot easily be described otherwise

pathetic fallacy the attribution of human feelings to objects in nature and, commonly, weather systems, so that the mood of the **narrator** or the characters can be discerned from the behaviour of the surrounding environment

plurality a large number of things, or ways of viewing a text

post-structuralism both a continuation and a critique of **structuralism**. Post-structuralist criticism expands the possibilities of language: the binary oppositions central to a structuralist position proliferate into innumerable alternatives. In post-structuralist readings meaning is never stable and uncontrovertible, but always provisional and contradictory

pseudonym an adopted name under which to write

psychoanalytic criticism a way of considering texts in terms of the psychoanalytic theories of Sigmund Freud. Emphasis upon dream analysis. Later psychoanalytic theory takes account of the work of Jacques Lacan, especially his theories of language

Romantic a literary form characterised by a conscious preoccupation with the subjective and imaginative aspects of life

semiotics the study of signs and sign systems. Associated particularly with the work of Ferdinand de Saussure

structural opposition from the teachings of Ferdinand de Saussure. Saussure's general conclusion is that 'in a language there are only differences, without positive terms'. In other words, meaning comes from difference and does not occur in the terms themselves. The differences are conceived of as structural oppositions, i.e. we understand cold because it is not hot

structuralism structuralist criticism derives from the linguistic theory of Saussure. It focuses on the internal structures of language which permit a text to 'mean' something. A structuralist analysis posits language rather than an individual author as the creator of meaning: no word has intrinsic meaning, in and of itself – it only means something in relation to other words. This insight is discussed chiefly in terms of binary oppositions. We understand what 'hot' means only in relation to the term 'cold'. According to structuralists, writing has no origin – every individual utterance is already preceded by language

sublime quality of awesome grandeur, as distinguished from the beautiful, in nature

symbolic, symbolism investing material objects with abstract powers and meanings greater than their own; allowing a complex idea to be represented by a single object

transcendent often synonymous with metaphysical – that which is beyond the limits of human knowledge; exceeding or surpassing the ordinary

TIMELINE

HISTORY	AUTHOR'S LIFE	LITERATURE
1825 First passenger railway opens	**1818** Born in Yorkshire the fifth of six children	**1811** Jane Austen, *Sense and Sensibility*
1834 Parish workhouses introduced. Abolition of slavery in territories governed by Britain	**1821** Her mother dies and she is sent to Cowan Bridge School as a boarder	**1817** Lord Byron, *Manfred*. Sir Walter Scott, *Rob Roy*
1837 The Victorian era begins. Victoria becomes queen	**1825** Emily's two elder sisters die of consumption at Cowan Bridge School and Emily and her sister Charlotte return to Haworth where they are brought up by their aunt	**1818** Mary Shelley, *Frankenstein*. Lord Byron, *Childe Harold* (Canto IV)
1838–42 Chartism is at its peak of popularity		**1819–24** Lord Byron, *Don Juan*
1842 Employment in mines of women and children under ten is outlawed. Chartist uprising	**1835** Attends Roe Head School to study to become a teacher but is physically homesick and returns to Haworth	**1830** William Cobbett, *Rural Rides*
		1838 Elizabeth Barrett Browning, *The Seraphim and Other Poems*
	1837 Spends six months as a governess at a girls' boarding school at Law Hill near Halifax, before returning home because of ill health	**1848** Robert Browning, *Dramatic Lyrics*
		1857 Elizabeth Gaskell, *The Life of Charlotte Brontë*
	1842 Goes to Brussels with Charlotte but aunt dies and they return home	
	1846 Emily and her sisters publish a book of poems under the pseudonyms Currer, Ellis and Acton Bell	
	1847 *Wuthering Heights*	
	1848 Brother Branwell dies; Emily dies from tuberculosis	

REVISION FOCUS TASK ANSWERS

TASK 1

Lockwood is an unreliable narrator.

- There is a discrepancy between Lockwood's narrative and Nelly Dean's: for example, his first analysis of the character of Heathcliff.
- Lockwood's inability to read landscape, both literal and social, suggests a limited viewpoint.
- Lockwood tends to jump to conclusions about both character and situations: Heathcliff, Cathy, the pile of rabbits. This shows his lack of awareness, sensitivity and judgement.

Wuthering Heights and Thrushcross Grange represent two completely different ways of seeing the world.

- There are contrasting descriptions of both the houses and the characters: refined/rustic; civilised/wild.
- There are differences in the treatment of women: Catherine and Cathy, and Isabella.
- Faith and religion: Joseph has a puritanical and punitive view of religion; Edgar Linton has a tolerant and hopeful view of faith, but this can be compared with his vindictive and judgemental reaction to Isabella.

TASK 2

Consider the importance of repetition in *Wuthering Heights*.

In an essay requiring you to analyse repetition it is particularly important that you set out your argument clearly. Here are some suggestions for areas to cover:

- Names and characters, i.e. the ways in which the same characteristics have different impacts in different generations.
- Abduction/imprisonment: i.e. Catherine at Thrushcross Grange; Cathy at Wuthering Heights.
- Imagery: animals; whips, guns and knives; literature and books.

Consider the importance of dreams and the supernatural in *Wuthering Heights*.

- Lockwood's dreams at Wuthering Heights are vivid and powerful, and give us clues to the main themes and plot while adding greatly to the tension and atmosphere.
- Catherine's dreams about heaven reveal her subconscious desires.
- Ghosts: Lockwood's dream of Catherine; the final image of the novel when the little boy sees the ghosts of Catherine and Heathcliff on the nab.

TASK 3

Consider the importance of religion for this novel.

Consider:

- The character of Joseph: his puritanical approach
- The religious sensibilities of Catherine and Heathcliff and how they contrast with conventional religion
- Edgar Linton's view of religion and his behaviour towards Isabella and Catherine
- Nelly Dean's view of religion

Discuss the relationship between class and empathy in *Wuthering Heights*:

- Lockwood's relationship with Nelly Dean and the residents of Wuthering Heights shows his pomposity and lack of empathy.
- The character of Catherine and the impact of her experiences at Thrushcross Grange show the contrast between the Heights and the Grange and Catherine's transformation.
- The relationship between Cathy and Hareton suggests empathy and love can triumph over class.

TASK 4

Emily Brontë's representations of nature are always symbolic.

Consider:

- The descriptions of the moors and landscapes which can be seen as both symbolic and literal
- The use of animal imagery
- Heathcliff and Catherine's experiences of the landscape

In *Wuthering Heights* madness is portrayed as a dysfunction of society, not of the mind.

Consider:

- Catherine's brain fever
- Hindley's deterioration
- Heathcliff's derangement after Catherine's death

MARK SCHEME

Use this page to assess your answer to the **Worked task**, provided on pages 104–5.

Aiming for an A grade? Fulfil all the criteria below and your answer should hit the mark.*

> **'In *Wuthering Heights* death is seen as a welcome release from the tortures of living.'** How far do you agree with this view of the novel?

A01 — Articulate creative, informed and relevant responses to literary texts, using appropriate terminology and concepts, and coherent, accurate written expression.

- You make a range of clear, relevant points about death and the torments of life in *Wuthering Heights*.
- You state your position clearly, i.e. whether you agree or disagree with the statement.
- You use a range of literary terms correctly, e.g. **palimpsest**, theme, **Romantic**, **Gothic**.
- You write a clear introduction, outlining your thesis, and provide a clear conclusion.
- You signpost and link your ideas about death, release, the afterlife and the torment of living.

A02 — Demonstrate detailed critical understanding in analysing the ways in which structure, form and language shape meanings in literary texts.

- You explain the techniques and methods Brontë uses to present death, the afterlife, heaven and haunting and link them to main themes of the text.
- You may discuss, for example, the description of Catherine's death and the impact it has on both Heathcliff and Edgar.
- You explain in detail how your examples affect meaning, e.g. the way Heathcliff pins himself to the tree with grief when he learns of Catherine's death can be read as a crucifixion, thus figuring Heathcliff as a Christ-like figure rather than a demon.
- You may explore how the settings – in particular the graveyard and the moors – contribute to the presentation of death and the relationship between Heaven and Earth

A03 — Explore connections and comparisons between different literary texts, informed by interpretations of other readers.

- You make relevant links between death and release, life and suffering , noting how the expression of the latter is undermined by the expression of the former.
- When appropriate, you compare responses to death and a belief in an afterlife in the course of the novel with the way these ideas are represented in other text(s), e.g. the way that, in *Frankenstein*, Victor pillages graveyards, and how he deteriorates when another of his friends or family members is killed.
- You incorporate and comment on critics' views of how death and redemption are presented in the novel.
- You assert your own independent view clearly.

A04 — Demonstrate understanding of the significance and influence of the contexts in which literary texts are written and received.

You explain how relevant aspects of social, literary and historical contexts of *Wuthering Heights* are significant when interpreting expressions of love, desire, grief and death. For example, you may discuss:

- Literary context: Heathcliff presents himself in the role of the isolated and alienated Romantic hero-villain.
- Historical context: Heathcliff's use of the inheritance laws to further his own security in life.
- Social context: How each character responds to death is partly the result of class, religious sensibility and social decorum.

* This mark scheme gives you a broad indication of attainment, but check the specific mark scheme for your paper/task to ensure you know what to focus on.